MIDDY
BROWN'S
JOURNAL III

MIDDY BROWN'S JOURNAL III

A Time for Everything

A novel By M. Louise Smith

iUniverse, Inc.
Bloomington

MIDDY BROWN'S JOURNAL III
A Time for Everything

iUniverse books may be ordered through booksellers or by contacting:

iUniverse
1663 Liberty Drive
Bloomington, IN 47403
www.iuniverse.com
1-800-Authors (1-800-288-4677)

ISBN: 978-1-4759-6993-1 (sc)
ISBN: 978-1-4759-6994-8 (hc)
ISBN: 978-1-4759-6995-5 (ebk)

Printed in the United States of America

iUniverse rev. date: 1/18/2013

www.mlouisesm.com

There is an appointed time for everything,
And in due season, all things pass under heaven;
A time to be born and a time to die;
A time to plant, and a time to pluck up that which is planted;
A time to kill, and a time to heal;
A time to break down, and a time to build up;
A time to weep, and a time to laugh;
A time to mourn, and a time to dance;
A time to cast away stones, and a time to gather stones together;
A time to embrace, and a time to refrain from embracing;
A time to get, and a time to lose;
A time to keep, and a time to cast away;
A time to rend, and a time to sew;
A time to keep silence and a time to speak;
A time to love, and a time to hate;
A time of war, and a time of peace,

He hath made every thing beautiful in its time. He hath also set the world in every heart. No man can find out the work that God has made for him from the beginning unto the end. Wherefore, I perceive that there is nothing better than that a man should rejoice in his own works, for that is his portion.

Ecclesiastics: 3

CHAPTER ONE

▼

"Madge, Madge! I don't know who else to call . . . Please, get over here as fast as you can! Madge . . . . ?"

I cradled the phone while I rolled over and looked at the clock. Four-thirty in the morning in the middle of a blood-freezing December storm that since midnight, had been howling and whipping out it's agony outside my condo in Denver, Colorado. I moaned. It took me a few seconds to push away the cobwebs and recognize the voice, "Mac, what's happened, where are you . . . are you all right?"

He was breathless and his words spilled over one another. I sat bolt upright and asked him to repeat slowly . . . surely I had misunderstood.

"Madge, a body, a frozen body, and the police are here, I didn't know who else to call . . ."

I took a deep breath, now fully awake. "I'm on my way; where are you, Mac."

"The church, by the grotto, she's dead."

✳　　　✳　　　✳　　　✳

Dead indeed; eerie flashing lights splashed across the trodden snow periodically illuminating the slight hump that roughly outlined a human form. Huge technicolor flakes of snow swirled silently around the crime scene tape in a futile attempt to convince me that I must still be dreaming. I stood at the outer perimeter of the small gathering of Denver's Finest until Mac . . . Father Dominick Francis McMullen . . . caught sight of me and stumbled through the knee-deep snow. He all but collapsed into my arms.

"Madge, it's that Mahoney woman, the one . . . ."

"Dear Lord! Mac, catch your breath, don't have a stroke here on me . . ."

I pulled off my down jacket and wrapped it around the thin, convulsing shoulders of my old parish priest and long time friend. He was bent under the weight of his saturated woolen bath robe and his sparse hair was plastered to his head.

"How long have you been out here . . . Mac, for heaven's sake, let me get you inside the rectory you'll catch your death out here;" an unfortunate choice of words at best.

During our brief encounter I had already begun to shiver and my clothes were rapidly becoming snow-clogged. I maneuvered Mac back toward the circle of police who had now been joined by a police photographer overseeing the process of having the snow gently brushed from the rest of the body.

I work on a part-time basis for one of Denver's outstanding private investigators and in the course of my involvement, or interference, as I honestly admit is sometimes more an appropriate description, I've seen more than my share of bodies. I had a speaking acquaintance with some of the local officers and our own part-time office assistant at *C.C. Investigations* was Police Officer Darcy Davenport. I recognized the tall, lank frame of Crime Scene Investigator Bart Cannon and left Mac long enough to shuffle over. "Cold night for a call, Bart, what do we have here?"

He grunted. "Well, from the unnatural position of the head, I'd guess it'd be pretty hard to break your own neck and make it this far before you collapsed."

"Murder . . . Oh God, poor Mac. Who found the body?"

He nodded toward a dark figure hunkered down on a stone bench near the far side of the grotto. "Says he's the handyman, come in early to set up for morning Mass. We got the call just over half an hour ago." He jerked his head toward Mac who was nodding in response to one of the officers. "Looks like you know the poor old fellow."

"Father Mac, yes, we've been friends for a long time. He's pretty upset, understandably, okay if I take him across to the rectory?"

Bart glanced around and leaned closer. "You can try, but from the statement of the handyman, your pal could be in a bit of trouble; seems he had quite a set-to with the victim last night."

I stood on tip-toe and saw the body for the first time, glowing in a portable lamp held by a rotund figure in a tartan plaid topcoat. Yeah, I knew the woman. She and Mac had had more that a few "set-to's" in the past. She was the head of an off-shoot feminist radical group that called themselves *Magdalene*. The last time Mac had mentioned it he said he was fed up with the constant struggle of wills because the Mahoney woman demanded to have the pulpit during Mass to "inform" the congregation of their findings and the so-called *Mary Magdalene Conspiracy*. Their claim to dubious fame was their insistence that there had never been an *Apostle John, Beloved of Christ*, he was just John a disciple and Mary of Magdala, or *Mary Magdalene* was actually the *Beloved of Christ*. Variations and varieties of that theme had been beaten to death from the printed page to the Internet. I was a bit confused about the topic and media hype; but they purported to have scriptural proof that one-time writers of the early Scriptures, men of course, had invented and elevated John's position and degree of importance to Christ when in reality the favorite disciple had always been *Mary Magdalene, Beloved of Christ*, a prolific writer and composer of *the Gospel of Mary*. They claimed that she was also wife of Jesus, mother of his children and his teaching companion. It wasn't just their recent platform, I remember Mac sharing his frustration regarding this group long before George and I ever separated, which was now well over three years ago.

As a matter of fact, it was because of my relationship with my private investigator boss, Calvin (Cal) Cleere, that I had become regrettably but somewhat well known in the law enforcement community and a major reason George had had quite enough of his wife, Madge Middleton Brown. As for myself, I'd overcome the empty-nest syndrome when my son, George Jr., Geo (pronounced Joe,) and daughter Pam subsequently went off to college by becoming a quite successful *StarWays* beauty consultant and the part-time P.I. assistant to Cal. Things have gotten out of hand on several occasions, of course. I don't pretend to always control my instinct or emotions but I'm very good at both of my careers.

Chauvinist ex-spouse George, convinced that I didn't have the brains to think my way out of a paper bag, found himself an intellectual, Internet *soul mate* in a fellow engineer, a-woman-thank-God, and had long been in the process of trying to divorce dumb little me. So, aside from my somewhat predictable romantic involvement with Cal, I'm a woman on my own with grown kids and a passion for almost everything. I did a re-write number on my given name, "Madge" by which Mac has long known me, and for several years have used almost exclusively my professional name, one that I feel suites me just fine; "Middy . . . Middy Brown" as derived from my maiden name, Middleton. But right now, *Madge* had to take care of Father Mac, and it wasn't starting to look promising.

With all the salivating press ready to jump on the first impropriety even remotely attached to a priest, I was aware that vultures had landed on the scene, beaks sharpened, tattered wings folded for the duration, and remote mikes at the ready. Side by side I propelled Mac as we slogged through the snow to the rectory. I pushed him inside, but not before a sharp series of flashes captured my backside for posterity.

I knew my way around the rectory and proceeded to make a pot of strong coffee in the tidy kitchen kept by Mac's faithful housekeeper, Carmen. The last time I'd been in the same kitchen I had been saddled with a killer posing as a nun, biting my nails in frustration as she snored in Mac's favorite recliner in the adjoining living room. Mac and I had narrowly escaped death that time, and now this. I'd sent Mac to his room to stand in a hot shower and thaw out. The man was a wreck. He had been talking retirement for months now. His sister had a condo in Florida that would soon be tenant free and he told her he'd consider taking it. It looked as though Fate just would not turn the poor man loose.

I carried my coffee to the window and looked through an opening in the blinds. Across the snow-covered grounds I could make out the coroner's van loading the body. Two reporters were camped out approximately five feet in front of me on the front steps yakking away on their cell phones, no doubt with the "Hold the Press" vigor one would expect from such as they in such a circumstance. This was a dreadful time for the parish to be in between associate pastors since the newly ordained Father something-or-other-Polish, had not yet taken yet up residence. Mac shouldn't be carrying the full load of the needs of the parish, especially Mass every morning in this crappy weather.

I paced the floor and tried to organize my thoughts. My first reaction had always been to call Cal. Not this time. Even if he hadn't been in a training program in D.C. with The Department of Homeland Security, I'd matured enough to learn how to avoid pushing the panic button unless I was really in over my head. From what C.S.I. Bart Cannon told me, I knew the first thing on the agenda, after hearing his comment about the "set-to" was to have someone put in a call to the Chancery office and have a Diocesan appointed attorney at the ready, ask for a loaner priest, and assign a spokesperson to make a statement to the Press. Since my name had been bandied about when that phony nun had splattered herself all over a farmer's corn field in Northern Colorado and I had been astraddle Mac's Harley behind him at the time of her demise, I didn't want the Chancery office to have reason to add me to the list of those who would rather not hear my name again. Obviously, I needed help. I would function as his body-guard and protector in the meantime, God knows he'd held my hand and helped me keep my sanity more times than I cared to recount.

★   ★   ★   ★

When Mac came into the living room, my heart sank. Gone was the robust, vigorously healthy man who in happier days had once jogged past our house on Saturday mornings and stopped in for coffee on the patio. Two heart attacks, a minor stroke, and a workload imposed by the diminished call to vocations had taken a horrific toll on my dear friend. He just shouldn't be expected to take any more. He'd been assigned a new parochial vicar almost annually to help oversee the school and various parish needs, but they'd been periodically pulled to fill in the rapidly accelerating attrition rate in parishes across the country. The responsibility of shepherding a parish of two thousand plus families and a school from pre-kindergarten to grade eight was a daunting task a much younger man would balk at undertaking. Mac was the faithful one, always back on his feet and ready to pick up the shepherd's staff and soldier on. Why didn't priests have wives to put their foot down and say *enough is enough already*?

He had pulled on a set of his clerics, the white collar slightly askew, and his black socks inside out. His hair was still standing on end from its quick encounter with a towel. He tried to smile but it was not going to make it as far up as his eyes, which were now looking anxiously at me. "Madge, how could this have happened, and what was Johnny doing on the grounds this time of the morning? He has instructions to stay at home in snow; he can't possibly maneuver himself on those prosthetics in this kind of weather! I wish he wouldn't be so dedicated to this job. He has a backup . . ." He collapsed into a kitchen chair and put his face in his hands.

I shrugged my shoulders, "He told the police he was here to set up for early Mass."

The tired priest shook his head, "Mass during the winter months is at seven. All he has to do is check the thermostat, turn on the lights, and unlock the doors; he could do that at 6:45 and still have time left over. He could have called in our part-time guy who is always standing by. I don't understand. The police said he told him about my shouting match with that Mahoney woman."

I sat down on the kitchen chair across from him, "Mac, no offence intended, but that Mahoney woman was a robust woman while you, my dear friend, are a worn out shell of a man who can scarcely push open the heavy main doors to the church anymore. Without being disrespectful to the dead, how in Heaven's name could you have possibly maneuvered her overly plump and extremely muscular bulk enough to even reach her upper body and then have her allow you to grab her around the neck, much less break it?"

He scrubbed his weary eyes with his fists for a moment. "The Bishop' office is going to have a hemorrhage. This is the second questionable death attached to the Reverend Dominick Francis McMullen within a short period of what, two years? He's probably going to start excommunication documents before he even gets off the phone . . . and worse, who is going to call him this time? Not me, for certain. I don't even know what to say to him."

Raising my eyebrows I quickly replied, "Nor me." I refilled his coffee cup and pulled a church bulletin off the cork-board beside the phone. Mac had three ordained deacons assigned to him to assist in serving the parish. Unfortunately, they ranged in age from sixty nine to eighty four. While they were commissioned to preside at funerals, baptisms, communion services and so forth, their combined energy levels were a bit askance. I perused the list of said deacons and punched in the number of Deacon Lou Peretti, a retired attorney. In a matter of minutes he arrived. I met him at the door as he was waving his hand to the accumulated Press. I scooted out of sight behind the door as he was holding up his hand with the standard, "No comment for now, thank you, sorry, no comment."

I had moved Mac into his place of solace, his big leather recliner, the one he had scarcely agreed to keep after the phony nun had occupied it for far too many hours that long nightmare ago. He was perched on the edge, his head hung down in his hands at knee level. When Deacon Lou came into the living room I took his coat and scuttled into the kitchen to get him a cup of coffee and leave them to their task.

CHAPTER TWO

— ▼ —

I shook out my down jacket, amazed that the "water repellant" label for once was somewhat accurate. I was pondering my escape method and decided to take the path of the greatest resistance and go out the back door, tromp around the outer perimeter of the grounds through the thigh-high snow drifts, and get to my car without falling within the view of the dwindling paparazzi when Mac called me to the living room. He motioned to the chair next to the sofa and I sat down.

"Madge, Lou and I would like to go over what we collectively know about Johnny, our maintenance manager cum handyman."

Deacon Lou spoke up, "From what I understand, he pretty much clamped the cuffs on Mac with his statement about Mac arguing with the dead woman last night."

Mac nodded his head, "the officer who was questioning me said that Johnny told him that I had repeatedly threatened the woman with expulsion from the building and that she had told me that she'd go to the Bishop 'again' if I gave her any further trouble."

I was certainly taken aback. "Go to the Bishop *again*, what's been going on that made him tell the police that?"

Mac reached for his coffee, looked into the cup and put it aside. "I don't know how it all started. Apparently the Mahoney woman had taken Johnny into her confidence. Her group has been growing and getting stronger all the time. They started out with only four or five women, then they asked for one of the meeting rooms downstairs at the church, and then she nagged me about wanting her own key so they could get in and out and promised they were responsible and would lock up. I'm sorry, I've had so much to do, I told Johnny to get one made for them about three months ago. I've pretty much lost track of them till she started hounding me again to let her speak from the pulpit about the *amazing facts* they had uncovered about the *true* Mary Magdalene. I told her that was out of the question on a variety of different levels on at least two different occasions, and of course in my state of mind these days, I unfortunately raised my voice last night and became quite agitated. I should have apologized later but couldn't bring myself to do it. They've become like unholy predators, encroaching everywhere, even putting flyers on a few cars in the parking lot which has caused no small amount of complaints. I've have our church secretary handle them so I wouldn't have to . . . I'm tired my friends, so very tired."

Deacon Lou gently turned to subject back to the handyman, "Now, how about this Johnny, he apparently did witness last night's exchange with the Mahoney woman."

Mac shrugged, "I'm certain it wasn't the only time either. That group has been harassing me and they think they're going to break me down and I'll give in to them again. As for Johnny, I've depended on him a lot and he's always delivered. In the course of events, I've given the boy pretty much free reign. I shouldn't call him a boy, he's a medically discharged or a retired Colonel, I'm not sure which's correct, maybe both. He's at least in his late forties, maybe early fifties, I don't remember. He's served three tours in Iraq and then one in Afghanistan. Seems like the military funerals we have around here are mostly results of that third tour. Johnny even went back for a fourth. I guess he's lucky only losing his legs and having multiple skin grafts from that IED that got to him. He's very quiet; I sense there is a very strong underlying pain that he's dealing with. That is certainly understandable what with the extent of his injuries and disabilities compared to his former military standing. He probably has a Purple Heart or at least a chest full of medals, but he's not the sort who would boast of it. He sighed, "I don't for a moment perceive him to be a danger to himself or others. He's been with us over a year and I honestly don't know why he would have even been around last night unless maybe he spent the night on one of the pews; as I said, he has a hard time getting around in deep snow with his double prosthesis. He's a bilateral amputee . . . prosthetic legs. He is very conscientious about his responsibilities and walks to work since he doesn't have a handicap-fitted vehicle. His mother was a parishioner until her death about six months ago and she used to drive him. He has a wife and grown daughters somewhere he told me rather unhappily. My take on it is when he came back from his fourth tour maimed and disheartened, he moved back home with his mother, not necessarily of his own volition. I think he's found a comfortable place here with us . . . always seemed mentally sound, took the loss of his mother pretty hard, understandable of course, a nice boy overall. That's the extent of my knowledge of him."

Lou stretched his shoulders and rotated his neck, his own weariness showing, "So you haven seen any signs of Post Traumatic Stress Syndrome or anything along those lines, has he worked well with people?"

"Always seemed to, oversees minor repairs, contacts contractors and gets bids for the financial committee; overall, I'm fond of him. Given all that he's been through; he's a somewhat reflective person and a nice Catholic fellow, former altar boy and all. He reads the *New Testament* sitting in the back of the Church sometimes and often asks me what I think of a certain passage, what it could mean, and so forth. He said his Bible was all that kept him alive during those multiple deployments, surgeries, and rehabilitation. I don't think he would deliberately 'clamp the cuffs' on me as you put it."

Lou rose, "Well, I'll wait until eight and call the Chancery office, I'll see if I can get a loaner priest and take you out of the picture until this mess is settled, you'll need them to assign an attorney as well and I'll write up a statement for the Press after I talk to the police and get the Archbishop's office to sanction releasing it. For now, there's nothing we can do. Let's give you something and put you to bed. Mrs. Brown, anything to add?"

I started out of my thoughts, "No, actually Carmen will be here in an hour or so, you might give her a call before you leave and give her heads-up. As for myself, I think it's time for me to head home. There's nothing I can do here other than offer my support to Mac. And by the way, put a note on the door of the church that Mass is cancelled until further notice. I'd suggest referring them to the Cathedral's schedule. Mac is going to need someone to oversee the church's physical needs, I think that Johnny fellow has a snow removal contractor; you might want to make sure they are set up to come as needed, not to wait for a call from the church. Winter has only just started. Who knows when even this storm will move out? Also, just looking ahead at the rental of the facilities; with Christmas coming we'll probably need to get someone in to make sure all those needs are either met or events cancelled." I ignored Mac's moans, "Obviously, this couldn't have happened at a worse time. I just don't know what I can do; I guess I can come over in the morning and work with the secretary for a few hours and see what's scheduled. We really need that fill-in priest immediately.

Mac nodded and wearily rose, his voice scarcely above a whisper, "Madge, there's something else; on my desk there's a large manila envelope, I only slit it open and added a couple of prior correspondence pieces, I didn't look at the other contents. You'll see that it's from George. Please go to my office and take it. I don't want to be further involved. Try to get through to him that I am no longer his parish priest and cannot be caught up in the middle of whatever is going on between the two of you. You know that *you're* always welcome to rely on our friendship and know that I'm always a sympathetic ear. I hold you in very high esteem and know you have problems of your own. However that said, I need you to work with the powers that be on this Mahoney thing tonight and am counting on you to be strong for all of us. I'm going to have to step down soon, that is if I'm not destined to spend the rest of my declining years behind bars."

✳   ✳   ✳   ✳

I drove home in a blue funk finding it hard to steer my new SUV. The roads were almost impassable and I followed a snow plow most of the way until I turned on to the quiet street next to the golf course and into the complex housing my cozy little condo. Without its four-wheel drive, I would have never made it away from the church grounds.

A few years back, at the end of my first year as a *StarWay* beauty consultant, I was incredulously awarded a beautiful fully loaded Cadillac sedan, an extraordinary prize that came to me as the outstanding consultant of the year. Of course, it had been a fluke that all those sales came about; I had only expanded upon the basic customer base I inherited when a current consultant had to discontinue working, and I seemed to have a knack for acquiring referral customers.

That said, I live in Denver, Colorado and Denver is the "Mile High" city . . . 5,280 feet above sea level, nestled against the Rocky Mountains and home to wintery snow storms that can bury the city practically over night. So with minor regret, I traded in the Caddie and went "native" with a sturdy, dependable four-wheel drive with award-winning traction. I'd never have made it out of many situations without this wonderful vehicle at my beck and call. The locations of several of my customers make it necessary trek into the valleys and hills beyond Denver. In addition, with my daughter Pam living with me and coming very near the end of her pregnancy . . . which is an entirely different and heartbreaking story . . . I wanted to be absolutely certain that I could get her to the hospital on time in the dead of a December winter.

The light was on in the living room when I let myself in, and Pam was sitting in the large recliner, propped and fully padded fully with an assortment of pillows, asleep with a book open on what was left of her lap. She was scarcely past her eighteenth birthday and had already made decisions regarding her life that I probably couldn't have made at my current age, which, oh my goodness, which was getting too near sixty to merit discussion. Tears welled up in my eyes. I didn't want to wake her; sleep had long been an elusive commodity for her. When I saw her innocence so unchecked at moments like this, I had to keep myself from calling George and raging at him anew.

This was the culmination of a series of events that would never allow me to even pretend to care for the father of my children. Just over three years ago, when George had suddenly announced that he'd found his intellectual counter-part in an engineering chat room and subsequently scheduled the moving van to transport him and all his worldly goods to Florida, our world fell apart . . . at least mine did. He proposed to lease a wonderful and dramatic Florida-ish apartment, let the kids furnish their own rooms to their hearts desire and spend their first summer together in vacation bliss while he diligently worked away in an excellent position made possible through his new relationship with "Naomi." He promised the kids that they would always have a home with him and as I said, told them to furnish their bedrooms in anticipation of many years of happy visits, or should they decide, they were encouraged to consider a permanent residency with dear old Dad, a 'with-it' Florida college scholarship, the beach, eternal sunshine, etc. etc.

Unfortunately, the bliss rapidly began to disintegrate. After his first summer, Geo opted to return to CU, the University of Colorado in Boulder to finish his degree rather than transfer to Florida, and Pam scarcely made it through her summer job the following year until all, excuse me, *Hell* broke loose.

At the end of his lease, George moved into Naomi's beach house where he kept 'separate quarters.' When the kids arrived for their second summer, the kids found themselves without those forever after cushy accommodations of the prior year. Instead, Geo was bedded down on the screened balcony and Pam given makeshift quarters with a curtain closing off her alcove for 'privacy.'

The frosting on the cake was Naomi's baby brother, Edison, *The Coach* a spoiled, indulged, irresponsible young man of thirty-something, who, during an alcohol infused house-party sponsored by dear old Dad and Naomi-the-wonderful, took my Pam at her father's instance for a 'walk on the beach.' *The Coach* managed to mix the date-rape drug in her cola drink and then he did just that. Pam stayed until near the end of the summer, keeping her secret in fear that her brother, Geo, would have done bodily harm to Edison, or vice-versa. Even then she feared that George would have had a great deal of difficulty believing what had actually taken place since *The Coach* and Dad had become such inseparable pals; to my current thinking, they were two jerks out to get all they could and damn if they gave a damn.

George had called me a month or so afterward, rather humbly I thought, telling me that Pam had sold her car and that he was shipping all of her things back to Denver. He gave number and time of her flight. He insisted that Pam had given him no reason for her sudden departure from Florida. When she arrived and settled in she told me about the pregnancy and the decisions she'd made regarding it. We promised one another that together, we'd get through this and move on with our lives.

I quietly turned down the light and left Pam sleeping. She seemed so peaceful it was difficult for me to even imagine how the next few months and even years would work themselves out.

CHAPTER THREE

▼

A bit of background is probably in order. When I first met Cal, it was the result of the delivery of *StarWay* cosmetics that his beautiful daughter, Samantha, had ordered. Cal had just arrived from New York City where he had closed his P.I. business and moved to Denver to begin a new life closer to his daughter, her attorney husband, and his new little grandson. Sam had gone shopping that day and Cal, babysitting, offered to pay for her order. Since there were several new products in the shipment, I felt I should see my customer in person. I came back later in the day and was 'coerced' into staying for a very pleasant and extended visit with frosty, cold cocktails during which time it became apparent that this incredibly handsome gentleman was actually flirting with me. Delightful!

Over the days and weeks that followed, during which time my recollection of the transitional progress of my life became somewhat muddy, Cal and I became very . . . extremely . . . close.

That fateful summer later, when Pam came back from Florida totally devastated, disheveled, desperate and had subsequently shared her horrific story with me, I held up well until I got her cleaned up, calmed, fed, and put to bed. I then slipped out and collapsed against Cal when he opened the door of his condo, two doors down from my own. When he dosed me up with a vodka or two and I was at last coherent, he reassured me that we would all work it out. I probably never realized how terribly I'd grown to depend upon his unwavering strength. Then he had shared that Samantha, his daughter, was likewise pregnant and also due to deliver in December. He convinced me to think only of how happy we would be with two new babies in the family for Christmas.

✳   ✳   ✳   ✳

Several years ago, my beloved sister, Matt, went through a devastating bout with breast cancer. This happened long before our mother and dad sold their Denver home, retired, and moved to the Texas Rio Grande Valley. As ill as Matt was during that time, Mother wandered about her wringing her hands, crying, and mostly making things worse, Dad just paced the hallway outside her room at the hospital, the treatment rooms, her bedroom, my house, the back aisle at church, and miles of outdoor walkways. The pain our parents endured was more devastating to their two daughters than the horror of the cancer itself.

I mention this because after all of the many passing years, Matt's complete recovery, our healthy lifestyles, and convincing our parents that they could move on with their retirement plans and we'd be fine in Denver; I'd been quite positive that I had dodged the cancer bullet. In spite of prayers, abundant faith, clean living, and all of the platitudes that accompany one's best efforts, *Fate* is a fearful predator, hovering always just outside the realm of our consciousness. As I say, *Fate* was waiting in the wings. Just when I had Pam settled back in Denver and was certain that her pregnancy was progressing normally; I discovered that my turn was upon me.

The details are not important and I surely don't expect anyone to want to know about them. I'll only share that shortly after coming to some sort of acceptance of Pam's dramatic and ongoing episode, my long-postponed mammogram and subsequent radiologist's report came back informing me that I had a number of abnormal areas that would require biopsies. One thing led to another which in turn, dictated that I make immediate arrangements for a bilateral mastectomy to be followed by breast reconstruction.

For the next months my medical situation turned my poor pregnant daughter into a full-time shuttle bus to hospitals and doctors, and then my twenty-four-seven care-giver following each surgery. Matt, always my consoler, confident, and helper convinced me that if at all possible we would spare our elder parents the knowledge of both my cancer . . . and Pam's pregnancy. Wisely, I acknowledged that I didn't have the strength to disagree.

I scarcely remember the entire trauma to my body, heart, mind, and soul. My relationship with Cal had been put on a somewhat uncomfortable hold, both because of dealing with the realities of the prognosis, and after my moral code regarding our unorthodox relationship got through to me. I was certain that any hope of a life with him had now become impossible. I'm aware of course, that any woman who has endured the same initial diagnosis can relate. Fortunately, I was finally, blessedly, assured that the cancer had been successfully removed and *at this point*, no further treatment would be required.

Unfortunately, I'd made what could have been a selfish step and for all intents and purposes, banned Cal from my life during my cancer trauma. I'd only allow Pam to give him faithful updates. I refused to be seen half doped-up with pain medications and Valium, (although some of my hallucinations were quite enjoyable,) with surgical drains, and a general corpse-like complexion. As a result it was some time before Pam shared Cal's sad news that Samantha had suffered a miscarriage and would not be able to have other children.

As soon as I'd been able to care for myself after my first surgery, Pam accepted an invitation from Cal's daughter, by this time they had become fast friends, and Pam spent her days as a nanny, caring for Sam and Daniel's little boy, Jason. She agreed to stay on until Sam recovered from her surgery and was once again able to face the world. After my second surgery several months later, which was less traumatic, Pam was able to resume her nanny duties and had become part of Sam's family. The love shared between them was mutual on all sides.

As a matter of record, I was just three weeks past my final surgery when Father Mac had telephoned me with his urgent four-thirty a.m. call.

I simply had to push aside all of the other clutter in my mind and my life and focus on my conversation with my very mature eighteen year old daughter. I had to maintain my emotional strength and pray that my brain cells would keep electronically zapping the right crisis-to-calm areas. I only had room for Pam on my mind, especially since she'd bravely told me that she had entered into a tentative agreement with Samantha and Daniel to make arrangements for the private adoption of her unborn baby. Further she wanted to remain on in residence as a full time nanny. The agreement would include a small salary and enough time off to complete her degree with all her expenses paid. She assured me it was all very legal and she would be able to care for her own child as a nanny. She said she could never completely feel it was her own as a result of the sperm donor who had so brutally forced himself upon her, but she would love the child, simply not as her own. Then, after the arrival of the baby, we would all sit down together and go over every facet of the situation and be certain we were in complete agreement. We would establish a time-line to give Pam enough hands-on experience with her circumstances to be certain she would be able to move forward with her life and be positive that she had made the right decision. I'd had little else on my mind since, even though I'd known at the onset that Pam would never consult to an abortion, and had been determined to place the child for adoption.

Pam and Samantha were both very happy that this would be a perfect solution. Pam also added that by having some degree of authority over the child, she would have the opportunity to instill good values and waylay any slight sign of its father's evil. Now that we were within days of delivery, the decision was that she would leave the hospital alone and stay with me for a few weeks. Samantha and Daniel would be with her for the delivery and take the infant directly to their own home.

CHAPTER FOUR

▼

I shrugged out of my jacket, hung it over the back of one of the bar stools to finish drying and tossed out the quick note I'd left for Pam. Sighing, I picked up the fat manila envelope Father Mac had given me and carried it to my desk. Once again, as I had done in the past, I wondered what it was that placed me again and again in the midst of a tumultuous emotional and physical tsunami. I turned on the lamp and sat down.

As I pulled out the contents, I heard Father Mac's words again, *Try to get through to him that I am no longer his parish priest and cannot be caught up in the middle of whatever is going on between the two of you.* I felt a twinge of conscience that his frustration was divided equally between the two of us.

The multi-paged document was another copy of the supposed divorce degree that I had earlier refused to sign as a result of the Pam situation and the fact that his charges were slanderous. I wasn't comfortable with the document . . . was it a lawsuit, an admission of my many sins, a divorce that made me out to be a wife-vampire, frigid? Motherzilla? What? I already had an attorney standing by to work me through this, but I'd let George spend the last year doing what he felt he had to do to get rid of me. He'd wanted the divorce and had shacked up with Naomi-the-wonderful, so as far as I was concerned, he could use his dime. I just wanted to protect myself and my children when it got down to the wire and I didn't care how long it took. Let him sweat.

Clipped to the top was a note from George; *Father Mac, Please do all that you can to get Madge to sign these papers and let us put this mess behind us. Gratefully, George*

I looked at the dates of the two envelopes that Mac had slipped inside, noting that he had never said anything to me about receiving them. The first was dated in September.

Dear Mac,

I'm sure by now that Madge has confided in you. She is threatening to sue me for our daughter, Pam's, pregnancy, sighting child endangerment, neglect, breach of parental obligation, breach of promise, and another bundle of ridiculous charges. I'm not quite sure how to handle this. She sent the last papers back asking for a settlement that she will accept for Pam; five hundred thousand dollars, and then she will take her own divorce documents to her own attorney and get this over with. In addition, she, and I'm sure with the help of that private investigator she works for, have managed to have the local police pick up my friend's son for DNA testing. Not surprising, Pam has refused to have the DNA of the unborn child tested until after its birth.

Now I know, being a man of the world that many girls during their first and subsequent years away from home and in college, will experiment with any number of forbidden fruits. My son's friend strongly denies having had any relationship whatsoever with my daughter and I believe him, unfortunately stifling Pam and Madge's plans to further pad their bank accounts, oh yes, Madge has financial demands of her own that I thought had been settled.

I have cooperated with Madge's selfish demands to bring the divorce this far by working with her on the sale of our house. I do not understand why she feels that she can continue to manipulate me in this manner. I cannot even be positive that Pam is pregnant or if it's another one of Madge's erratic ideas to punish me for finally getting away from her. Perhaps you could verify that for me.

As a Man of God, Father Mac, I'm certain you have worked through the unfair and fabricated manipulations of frustrated women before in divorce or annulment proceedings and can have some sympathy for me, since you are well aware of Madge's maniacal foibles. It is with great confidence and thanksgiving that I beg your assistance in bringing this divorce to a final close.

Regards,
George Brown

I had to lift my hand to my chin to push my mouth closed. I couldn't believe what I had just read, so I read it over again, three times. George, that Bastard . . . he was blaming my Pam! His own beloved daughter! I was too angry to cry. I hadn't ever wanted to go to court over this but now I was willing to walk across a bed of hot coals to put a gun to his head. Boy, that Naomi really had put her claws into him. I didn't recognize an even remote character of the man I had lived with, served, and had happily produced his children. How could I have been so blind . . . no, so *stupid* to have endured what I had. This was only proof to me that this had been no marriage. And how dare he keep involving Mac . . . Dear Lord! I don't know how the dear man could even look at me any longer, let alone say that he cares for me enough to call me, like he had done at four thirty a.m. this morning, to come to his aid. I hadn't even told him about Pam's pregnancy. I could only wonder what all he had read between the lines! I opened the second letter, dated the tenth of November, only last month:

Dear Father McMullen,

I received your brief note. I am sorry you feel that you no longer want to continue our friendship. I realize now that you and Madge are quite a formidable team and that I am pretty well helpless to move forward against the strong fortress the two of you present. It would be best for all of us if you would use your influence to get these divorce papers signed immediately. Otherwise, I fear you will be called upon to testify in any court proceedings that are most certain to come up. I hope Madge will be happy with the problems she has created for all of us.

Sincerely,
George Brown

With bitterness, anger, and a degree of determination I'd never felt before in my life, I picked up a memo sticky and wrote in a bold black permanent marker:

<u>Note to Self:</u> Call attorney. Prepare law-suit and criminal proceedings against Naomi-whatever and her son as soon as baby born and DNA established and <u>take action immediately</u>

I stuck the note to the base of my desk lamp, turned out the light, and spent the rest of the night in the darken living room across from my daughter, watching the gentle flames dance around the logs in the gas fireplace, and frantically praying for her.

*   *   *   *

I made coffee at seven-thirty in the morning and went back to my desk. Although I thought I'd keep the Father Mac thing to myself, I needed to hear Cal's voice. I poured the Father Mac story out, reigning in my frustration.

"Middy, good Lord! I'll be home at the end of the week, let me handle this for Father McMullen if there's something we can do for him. You stay put and take care of Pam."

As usual, I'd tried to give him my two cents worth, but he knew what I'd be saying and galloped on.

"Sweetheart, please stay in the background on this, have Darcy keep you posted on what the police have found out, and if they arrest Father Mac, I'll call my attorney and have him send over a criminal law specialist to check everything out. By the way, did you get in touch with the divorce specialist he recommended?"

"Cal, slow down, my mind is in enough of a muddle. First of all, I don't even know where to start with the Mac thing. I can visit with some of those women in that Magdalene group and see if I can get any info. Maybe they'll talk more freely to me than the police . . . ."

"NO! Middy, please back off. Look, I just need to stay here until I get this course finished and accept my assignment; I don't have a choice in the matter. This murder investigation will still be going on. We can wait until I get back to start digging. Even if they arrest Mac, they're not going to finalize anything. Maybe he'd be safer in custody anyway since we don't know who's prowling around the church. I sure as hell don't want you exposed; we've been over that in the past . . . Get my drift, Middy? Stay put, don't involve us at this time, let the police carry on and we'll talk when I get back."

I have to confess, he told me exactly what I wanted to hear. I'd been banged up and dragged around enough in the past by getting involved in something over my head; I needed someone to make me pull back. I'd keep in touch with Mac, but that was absolutely all. I checked on Pam again, took a warm shower and curled up in my wonderful down comforter and was asleep in seconds.

An hour later the phone woke me. Deacon Lou called. The long and short of it was that John DeBeers, the handyman, was being held on a possible charge of Murder One. He and Mac had arraignments in court at ten o'clock today. Father Mac had been taken into custody as an accessory.

I knew Cal would be out of pocket so I left a message on his cell. I also knew a an attorney would be assigned, but I asked Cal to have his guy call me and I'd give him what info I had and see if there would be any opportunity to help Mac. I didn't want to run down to the jail or be snapped up by the Press weeping (metaphorically) in court. If someone remembered a recognizable frontal picture of me or dug up my name after last night's photo opportunity of my backside and decided to run down other press notations I had managed to acquire, my name would be Middy Mud . . . *Be good to yourself, Middy, use your head*, I chanted, *be good to yourself and for once, use your head!*

CHAPTER FIVE

▼

Okay, so I couldn't ignore this latest news about the dual arrests and knew I had to ignore my best intentions. I took out a note card and started jotting down a few notes.

The Rules of the Church are extremely clear on the vetting process for potential employees. John DeBeers had surely passed all queries from State and Federal resources and records. Mac and his HR staff would never have hired him otherwise . . . or, did Mac go through the process or just make a ruling from his heart. The more I thought back over his comments to Deacon Lou, I had a feeling I knew the answer; Mac felt sorry for this tragically injured war vet. Now he could have this infraction come back to haunt him. I shuddered at the memory; he had allowed the manager of the school cafeteria to hire that murderous nun impersonator without doing a background check . . . that's what happens when you work a priest so hard you dull his sense of procedure.

My Note to self:

-How could DeBeer's statement so severely implicate dear old Father McMullen?

-Why at the arraignment did Johnny get slapped with Murder One, no bail.

_Is it good news that Father Mac had been able to post bail and only charged with accessory before the fact, whatever that meant.

-Who are the attorneys for DeBeers and Mac? Two for one? Probably not.

-Why was Father Mac released into the custody of one of the Church wardens, a Brother?

-What could have happened between the Mahoney woman and DeBeers that resulted in murder? Why does Mac fit in?

-What is with that Magdalene group in the first place? What do they hope to achieve? How many women are members?

Before I had even put down my pen, I had logged into my computer and started a search on Mary Magdalene. After perusing a few of the overwhelming links, it looked as though she just might be the second most important person in the Bible besides Jesus himself.

I stayed glued to the screen for what seemed like hours until around noon when I heard Pam beginning to stir. I logged off, thoroughly confused. I could see how a group of women such as the *Magdalenes* could have come up with their own interpretation of the person known as *Mary of Magdala*. Was she or was she not the woman who anointed Jesus with the oil and dried his feet with her hair and tears, was she the prostitute whom Luke calls a *sinful woman*. It is apparent, however, that she held a central position among all the followers of Jesus. I wondered now, in what capacity.

So many different accounts have been recorded, and as we all know, anyone can put anything on the Internet. The problem is trying to sift out the "facts." People unfortunately have the misconception that if it's on the Internet, it has to be true. Yikes!

I found a plethora of writings in far too many references to even scratch the surface. Surprising, many of them do connect in one fashion or another. I recommend it, *but keep an open mind . . .* she is a fascinating topic, *but what do we really, historically know about her?*

In several sources the importance of Mary of Magdala is emphasized because her name is mentioned first ahead of any other women in the scriptures. New to me is the theory that she was one of the two sisters of the Lazarus whom Jesus raised from the dead . . . the most famous sisters in the gospels and those closest to him; Mary and Martha.

There is a great deal of debate I discovered as I perused many different theories and writings regarding whether Mary of Magdala was in fact the "harlot" or sinner who was cured of the seven demons; the demons possibly being physical or medical afflictions, or if she was "demonized" by early church fathers in order to minimize any woman's active role in the life of Jesus. Many traditions indicate that Mary *of Bethany* (same Mary known as Mary of Magdala/Magdalene, whom some wrote that she was black,) was married to Jesus and could have been three months pregnant at the time of the Crucifixion. Also, other "researchers" believe that Mary Magdalene (or *Bethany*) had four children with Jesus; two daughters, Tamar or Damaris, who, according to the Acts of the Apostles Damaris later married Saint Paul; another daughter, St. Sarah, two sons, Jesus Justus, named after his father, his title meaning that he was the Davidian crown prince, and another one unnamed, born in March 44, AD. These births would indicate that a crucifixion conspiracy arose to cover up the "fact" that Jesus was rescued from the cross by friends, and the "Crucifixion" story or tradition, was invented to cover up this escape, while Jesus continued to thrive elsewhere and continue as a faithful husband and continued to father children. I must add that in the Jewish tradition, apparently marriage for a "Rabbi" was required; it would have been extremely unheard of for a man of Jesus age and calling to remain single. Did you know that one "expert" who examined photos of the Shroud of Turin has tried to prove that a wedding ring is clearly visible on the left hand of the crossed hands of Jesus in his death shroud?

I shook my head in amazement hardly able to follow the page; Mary Magdalene, a good Jewish woman and his wife, grew to be in complete opposition to Jesus in the method of spreading this new faith, believing that Jesus had betrayed their cause and preached only salvation through Heaven. She separated from him and Saint Paul, a former Pharisee (legal power) carried out the divorce in accordance with his own beliefs and authority. Paul then officiated at the second marriage of Jesus when he married Lydia . . . more to follow on that one I hope! Whew! Who was it that said "If it's on the Internet it has to be the truth?!" Good Lord!

I had developed a headache! I'd have to pursue the Internet further now, just for my own edification and comedic entertainment. Obviously I had to quit skipping over these strange research *experts* and go back and dig for more *factual* sources and read the fine print. No wonder these church women had so easily drawn their own conclusions in forming their powerful little group. With all the written word, I really would like to know what part of their beliefs and research set off poor John DeBeers, since he apparently had confessed to the murder of the Mahoney woman; which took me back to why was Mac arrested?

Instinct rushed into the forefront of my mind, a sound from the other room . . . a groan . . . Pam was in difficulty, it was time. I hurried into the living room to find her kneeling on the floor in front of the recliner grabbing one of the pillows she had been holding . . .

She moaned, "Mom, Help!"

I ran to the window. Just as I had long feared, she'd gone into labor and we were in a full-blown blizzard, what to do first? I had to get her wrapped up fast and down the stairs to the garage . . . should I go down and warm up the car first, call the doctor, have her lie down, grab her suitcase . . . . reason prevailed; time the contractions and yank on some warm clothes and snow boots. I couldn't go in my robe and pajamas.

With my watch now in my hand, I sat on the floor next to her and held her and we waited till the next contraction had passed. I helped her to the sofa, her water hadn't ruptured. I noted the exact second and ran for a cold washcloth and put it on her forehead. The next contraction came at fifteen minutes. I called the doctor, he said we should get to the hospital now due to the storm or call an ambulance; he'd phone in to prepare the hospital for her arrival. Pam didn't want an ambulance. It took exactly ten minutes to get her loaded in the car and then the next contraction hit . . . twelve minutes. I pushed in four-wheel drive and started praying and backed out into the storm while she doubled up in pain.

The roads were constantly being plowed, thank you Denver. We slid a few times, but no damage to auto or patient and I pulled into the ER in record time. Pam was rushed up to labor and delivery. I parked the car, grabbed her suitcase, tried to keep from exploding while I presented the pre-admit papers to the very slow clerk at the admissions desk, and at last ran to the elevator and stuck my foot in the door that was trying to close.

I found her in a room with a nurse beside her. Pam smiled like she was in for a party. "I called Sam. She's on her way over." I tried to appear composed and calm.

The nurse smiled, "We have some time to wait, looks like we'll be here for a few hours, perhaps. With a storm like the one we're having, this is the safest place for her." She patted Pam's arm, removed the blood pressure cuff, and checked the fetal monitors. It was easy to see that the little tough kid inside was strong and doing fine. The nurse clipped the call button onto the sheet next to Pam and smiled at me. "This is going to be harder on you than on our patient or baby. You might want to grab a book and settle in. Can I bring you anything?"

I smiled, "I've had two of my own, I really just wish she'd get up and let me do it for her!"

The nurse laughed and Pam smiled, "It's my turn, Mom, you've already had yours," and then she doubled up in another contraction. The nurse turned back and gently laid her hand on Pam's tense abdomen and watched the monitors "Breathe deeply now, that's good, try to relax and let it pass. Try not to push; you're doing fine, just fine."

When the contraction passed, Pam had tears of pain running down her cheeks; she tried to smile, "Mom, I might let you do this after all."

Agonizing hours later, I stood by while Pam closed her eyes from the effort of her long labor and delivery and took Samantha's hand, "I want you to cut her cord."

Samantha was crying so hard that she only nodded and took the scissors from the doctor. Daniel, Samantha's husband stood next to me and I don't think either of us realized that we were caught up in a firm embrace. We released one another and I took Pam's hand as the nurse placed the perfect little girl on the scales and measured her. "Six pounds eight ounces, sixteen inches long; perfect in every way, you've done a very good job."

Pam nodded and moved her IV aside and turned her face to smile at me. "It's over, Mom. Can we go home now?"

The doctor stepped over and took her hand, "Stay with us a couple of days; you don't want to go home in this storm. Maybe it will hang around long enough to leave us a White Christmas. You'll be up and strong by then and out in the mall with all the other shoppers." He patted her hand and turned to me, pulling his mask off over his head. He raised his eyebrows and gave me a sad smile. I took his hand in both of mine and couldn't get the simple 'thank you' out. He nodded in understanding and left the room with one backward glance at Dan and Sam who were holding their new daughter and bursting with tears of joy.

The couple left with the nurse and baby to move her tiny little self into the newborn nursery where she would stay until cleared to go to her new home. When Pam was able to be moved, she was placed in a private room on the surgical floor.

CHAPTER SIX

▼

Two days later I was sitting in the hospital cafeteria having a cup of latte while waiting for Pam to get checked out and dismissal instructions leveled. I'd explained to the doctor that I have a weekend home in the country about an hour and a half from the hospital and wanted to know if he thought it would be safe to take Pam away for the Christmas Holiday. He readily agreed that as long as the roads were passable and she'd be safe from too much joggling around, that he felt it would be an excellent idea to give her a change of scenery.

The sun had been shining since the day before and I felt confident that opening up Mosscreek for Christmas was going to be a good idea. I'd boldly told Cal that I felt he should leave Sam and Dan alone with their little son and new baby daughter to establish their own tradition for their first Christmas together. He readily agreed and thus would be going to Mosscreek with Pam, Geo, and yours truly. I knew there would be some antique Christmas decorations in the attic and it would be fun to have a real country Christmas. I'd call him and tell him it was all set.

Again, a bit of a background; for some completely unknown reason, I met a lovely elderly poetess during my *StarWay* sales visits and she immediately developed a deep affection for me which immediately became mutual. Her name was Clarissa Bonforte and she was spending her final days in the care center/home where I had several customers. Simply by chance, when I met her I told her how very much I had always loved her work and that as a young girl I had all of her books, which were unfortunately destroyed in one of nature's disasters. She immediately gave me all of her first editions and said I was the last person on earth who even remembered her. After her death, her attorney asked me to pay a visit, and much to my dismay and surprise, she left me her family home, *Mosscreek*, along with enough money in trust to care for it, make repairs, pay taxes, and keep on her two caretakers, the dear old Haggis couple who lived in the gate house.

This was during those horrific and tumultuous times when George's escape from me was just coming to a showdown. Simple me, I had no idea at the time that he had long been planning his flight to wonderland with his Naomi and that this inheritance was going to seriously disrupt his well laid plans for dumping me and keeping his tax structure in tact. He demanded that I not accept this inheritance . . . yeah, right, like I'd give up a beautiful old country estate not far outside Denver in the beautiful, forested foothills just for a cranky husband!

Everything was falling apart for me and seemed to continue to do so for the ensuing endless months. I'd only been to Mosscreek just a few and far between times. Matt and I spent a weekend there, Cal and I spent some time doing repairs in and out, but neither of the kids had been there. When George started his shenanigans I immediately put this inheritance into a trust for Pam and Geo. I wanted to make sure dear George and wonderful Naomi would never get their grappling hooks into it. I'd sadly left its tender and loving care to the Haggis couple. It was time I made some serious decisions about it and this prolonged Christmas trip might just do the trick.

I'll mention here my successful career as a top *StarWay* beauty consultant. I had received many awards, as earlier mentioned, my lovely blue Cadillac having been one. Until my marriage, or lack thereof started infringing into every aspect of my waking and sleeping hours, I had loved every minute that I spent with my customers, even though a couple of them pulled me into deep yogurt with them, causing poor Cal and myself no small amount of grief.

When I had to deal with George and then Pam's horrific rape and ensuing pregnancy, I flew to *StarWay* headquarters and took along my book of business. Together with my regional managers, we came up with a plan to spread out some of my customers and assign them to other Denver representatives. I hated to leave the people I loved, but I met with each individually along with the new rep and had somewhat peaceful closures. My income dropped drastically, of course.

When I received my cancer diagnosis, again I asked to be released from my customers; this time, the remainder of them. I took a long-term medical sabbatical. When I was comfortable with myself and had regained my stamina, I went back to work for Cal, three-quarter time instead of the sporadic office presence I had put in before, and I walked away from *StarWay*. If I had been given a warning, or been taught a lesson about managing my life, I was going to pay attention this time.

When I talked to Cal about the Christmas in the country idea he dropped a small but interesting bomb on me. He said he was having me vetted so I could help him with his new Homeland Security position. He added that we'd have to let Darcy Davenport, our trusted cop cum secretary go at the end of the year, and would for all intents and purposes, close down the private investigator business. Our work would be such that Darcy could no longer be involved. I was sad to know we'd lose him and I'd have more to do, but at the same time, I was ready for a new challenging challenge. He said I'd have to go through a long application process in order to obtain a Security Clearance to stay on, and then I could keep being Della Street to his Perry Mason. It was an old silly thing we sort of hung on to.

He's always dropping some little bomb on me. This time he said he'd been brought on board and was an independent contractor for The Department of Homeland Security, and that he'd held his own Top Security Clearance for over eight years or so, and that he'd tell me about it all later. Well, it looked like I should most assuredly drop the *StarWay* phase of my life. In a way, George had been right when he once said that I was running the wheels off the old van. Looking back, I was running myself ragged, too, but it had been a darn good run.

Wow, I shivered; I'd have to be investigated by all the powers that be. I did a quick examination of conscious . . . I couldn't think of any sins of my past that would keep me from presenting a clean slate for the U.S. Government. Just in case, I'd better keep my *StarWay* sample case up to date.

*   *   *   *

My cell phone rang and it was Pam, calling from her hospital room upstairs, "Mom, Mr. Cooper (Pam's attorney) just called. The results of the DNA parental test on the baby matched perfectly to Naomi's son. Mr. Cooper had the lab send the results to Florida yesterday, and to the attorney Cal had involved there. They had the legal findings from the lab hand delivered to Dad and Naomi with a signature of receipt required. There is a 99.99% guarantee that that creep is the father. Mr. Cooper said it was tested twice, certified witnesses were present at both sample gatherings, and it will hold up in court if we want to pursue it. Mr. Cooper said we could go ahead with the statuary rape case he wants to compile."

I sighed, "I'm sorry we had to go through all of this honey, but this, unfortunately gives us the material to pursue what you wanted. We'll make an appointment with him next week and go over what course of action you decide to take. Are you ready to go home?"

"Not yet, I'm going to have to stay until the doctor sees me again, they said it should be within the next couple of hours. They just brought me lunch, so I think I'll rest after I eat."

I rang off and sighed, thinking of George's corrosive letters that Mac had given me. I wondered if he slept well last night.

CHAPTER SEVEN

▼

The hospital cafeteria opened and I got in line and selected an entrée and a dessert. I knew after all of those months of suffering heart-burn and pregnancy acid-reflux, now hopefully over, that Pam would want pepperoni pizza delivered tonight. As I sat down, a woman I recognized approached with her own tray; it was the nurse who was with us during the better part of Pam's labor and delivery.

"Mrs. Brown, do you mind if I join you?"

"Oh, Shanna, of course not please do. You probably have another patient anxiously awaiting your return."

She smiled, "No, actually we just delivered, twin boys. I thought I'd break away; it's been a long night. "I stopped in to see Pam. She is a brave little girl, I so enjoyed my time with her. You must be very proud of her."

Of course I nodded in assent, "Yes, I never would have believed that my scatterbrained little high school band junkie would have become a young woman so very wise beyond her years. I pray she is able to make it through all of this without too much permanent damage."

The nurse smile, "I know I'm imposing, but I spent a lot of quiet time with Pam and I wanted to tell you that I know she will be fine. She told me about her decision regarding the baby right up front and after spending time with her, even through the pain, I know she will never waver."

I thanked her for her short visit, finished my lunch and went for another cold drink. While I'd appreciated visiting with the young nurse, it had only served to postpone my phone call to my son, Pam's brother, my dear Geo. I returned to my table. By now the room was fully occupied with staff and visitors busy with their chatter. I decided to leave off my tray and take my drink to one of the more private sitting areas. Geo answered on the first ring, and slightly breathless, "Mom, how's Pam?"

"She's fine darling, I wanted to tell you that all is in order for us to move ahead. The DNA results were sent to Florida and we have a 99.99% match, which we could classify as a perfect match. Her attorney is determined to pursue a statuary rape charge; she was seventeen at the time of the assault."

Geo swore, still breathless, I gathered he was on the run to somewhere, "Damn that bastard, I still wish you'd let me go back to Florida and beat the crap out of him."

This was an old argument, "Pam said he'd have beaten the crap out of you. She prefers to beat him in court. She's going to slap him with the statuary rape and demand he relinquish all parental rights to the baby so she can proceed with the adoption. Is this a bad time to call?"

"Oh, no, sorry, I was just coming back to the apartment from outside. It's cold, slick, and beautiful. You know how CU's campus looks under a blanket of snow. Is Pam taking all of this okay, she sounded so casual on the phone this morning."

"She's just anxious for all of us to get together at Mosscreek. When will you be coming home? I'd like to leave in about two weeks; hopefully it will have warmed up a little by then. Are you finished with your classes?"

He paused and I thought he'd dropped his phone, "Ah, I have to hang around another week or so. I should be there in plenty of time for Christmas. I want to give Pam some adequate recoup time. I agree about not seeing the baby till after the New Year. I want to make sure she has no qualms about what she's doing and it all works out. Damn, I'd hate to see her have to raise that bastard's kid. God, I hope this hasn't ruined her life."

My kids have they grown close during all of this mess . . . I guess everything has a silver lining, "We'll all get through this," I assured him, "I want a wonderful family Christmas. Cal needs to let Sam and Dan have their private time to get used to their little family, and I'm happy you don't mind that he's spending Christmas in the country with us."

"Oh, hell no; he's a great friend and I think we all need a nice getaway. He has made all the difference for Pam, getting some of those details out of the way to help her bring this mess to an end. Anyway, I'm anxious to see this place you've been hiding from us for so long. My mother has an estate . . . can you believe?" He laughed, "I'll give you a call tomorrow and see how she's doing. Love 'ya."

After we rang off I headed back to the elevators to tell Pam how happy I will always be that I'd been blessed with such great kids. I had a hard time believing that George had actually fathered them, but again, that virgin birth thing just didn't seem to fit . . . .

I smiled as the lift transferred me to the seventh floor. I wondered why I hadn't noticed before. My son had moved himself away from his father in a subtle way that had probably given him a more defined identity. Instead of carrying on as George Joseph Brown, Jr., I'd noticed in a couple of copies he'd mailed home from college, he was now signing, G. Joseph Brown. Geo . . . Joe, my own young man. A little quick arrow grazed my heart. Dear God, how many wounds and injuries had that man inflicted upon those he had promised to love and care for? The doors opened and I stepped aside for a wheelchair to enter. I walked down the hall to embrace another of his victims. Dear Lord, how was I going to keep it all together on my own?

CHAPTER EIGHT

▼

Cal and I were relaxing in our favorite intimate club in the basement of the D&F landmark clock tower in downtown Denver. It had been a very long time since I'd visited my *StarWay* makeover touchstone, *Salon Jorj*, but I'd spent the afternoon being pampered and afterwards had gone shopping for a new cocktail dress. I knew my efforts had been a success by the iced champagne bucket at Cal's elbow, the heartbreakingly tender look in his eyes, and the gentle way he held my finger tips in his hands. He lifted my hand to his mouth and deposited a light kiss. He smiled, "You're hiding your battle scars well tonight. You must be okay with what's happening with the divorce, and for that matter, with George in general, any news?"

I'd dreaded that question. As briefly as possible I told him about the envelope Mac had given me, its painful content, and how tragically sorry I was that our poor old priest had been caught up in George's madness. Pam had already given him an update on how she had been working with the attorney he'd connected her with in Florida and the lawsuit she planned to file against Naomi's son, Edison. "She's going for a full conviction for Statutory Rape and he suggested adding unlawful imprisonment or kidnapping. She was only seventeen and he, over thirty. I've gone off the deep end as well. I'm hoping to file my own lawsuit. I'm asking for $500,000 for Pam and trying for parental neglect, child endangerment, and anything else your man can come up with. I'm going for the juggler. I'll show you the pile of charges he's logged in about our marriage and my erratic behavior. He's had his parents back up his charges, but of course, what do they know? They'd do anything for their dear George. At least, he's not involved my relationship with you in any way except that you are finding me resources to ruin him."

Cal refilled my champagne flute, "Maybe we should fly down for a couple of days and meet with the attorney and get this thing resolved. We need a definite court date and a clear definition of the charges. This divorce must be settled. Considering what Pam's gone through, I would imagine that any judge would be very sympathetic to her and rule in her favor against that coach bastard. If George wasn't so determined to punish you for something he alone sees, a no-fault divorce settlement with some monetary provision for you and Pam would be the most sensible thing to do. As far as that Edison character is concerned, he should be locked up and forced to pay her restitution."

I agreed with him on all counts, but just didn't have the strength to confront George. I wanted him to go away and leave me alone. Of course, that was a very immature attitude. I smiled and took his hand, "Perhaps so, I'll give it some thought. I just want to have a quiet Christmas and get Pam back up and running. Has Sam told you how Pam has been caring for little Jason during her recovery?"

He looked a little guilty, "Yes, I've been very closely involved in the process. I've seen little Victoria, she is beautiful. I'm sure you know what this means to Samantha and Daniel and little Jason as well. He's crazy about her and keeps trying to put his toys in the crib next to her."

I couldn't keep the single tear from sliding down my cheek. He dabbed it away, I smiled, "and Pam's been so brave. Do you think she can actually become a nanny to her own child? I know how very much she loves Sam's family. She's always said that God wanted her to have the baby for some special person. Cal, you know Pam, can she really function in that role without regret?"

He shrugged and refilled our glasses, "I don't know for certain of course, no one can make that call; I hope she can for Sam's sake. I know how desperately Pam wants to get her degree and make a life of her own. You know, if she'd been cold hearted and selfish she would have had an abortion and no one would have blamed her, but she stood by her convictions and said she knew as soon as Sam miscarried that she was simply God's instrument to provide the baby they so wanted. That it is a little girl almost proves her theory. Sam now has a perfect little family. I pray God allows them to live in health, peace and harmony for all of their lives, and I think Pam will always be involved; as will we. It's you I worry about. This has all been hell for you. I wish I knew what I could do to make it easier. You know I love you, deeply, don't you? I'd move heaven and earth to keep you safe and happy?" Before I could burst into sobs he took my hand and led me to the dance floor.

✳   ✳   ✳   ✳

We were far enough into the foothills at Mosscreek that the snow was still deep, sparkling white, and breathtaking. Pam was bundled up in her ski clothes and wrapped in and sitting on blankets. Geo was pulling her on the old sled they'd found hanging in the garage. It was the high-railed old-fashioned kind with a tall curved back and wooden side arms. Cal was out in the workshop next to the garage with Benny Haggis building a stand for the heavy Christmas tree they'd cut down from just beyond the hill behind the house. Gracie and I had finished lugging down the bags and boxes of the decorations from the attic that she assured me Miss Bonforte put up every year. She was pink with joy and excitement and had quickly added a well-worn but newly laundered and ironed apron over her soft flowered dress, intent on baking Holiday treats.

How could I possibly be so happy? My children were behaving as though they were six and ten years old again. We had wonderful people to take care of my new home, Benny and Gracie Haggis; what darlings. How I could be so fortunate? I was standing in a magnificent house that only through the incredibly gracious manipulations of God in Heaven was now mine. I was surrounded by people who loved me, yes, I acknowledged, *really loved me!* I put aside any thoughts of what I may have to face in the future. I saw Geo help Pam out of the sled and then he moved out of my line of site. He soon reappeared with Cal and Benny half dragging, half carrying the ultimate evergreen tree across the front yard. The front door opened and Pam's laughter sounded like the happy tinkling of the Waterford crystal goblets, polished and ready for toasting in the antique hutch. I put down my heavy coffee mug and hurried to help. Poor Gracie couldn't decide if she should help or put on the hot chocolate. In the end, we all ended up covered with the accumulated snow from the deep branches, wet and cold, but oh, so very happy. Cal caught my eye and sent a silent kiss. My heart was near to bursting.

We insisted that Gracie and Benny have our Christmas Eve dinner with us. I'd brought along ingredients to prepare a couple of favorite dishes that I'd learned from a dear chef friend, *Stan the Man,* and they'd been quite a hit with my children. Cal and I sent the Haggis' home and the kids off to the upstairs TV room to enjoy a Christmas Eve with MTV. Cal and I, in between some really sweet knoodling, did up the dishes and retired to the old parlor in front of one of the fireplaces to enjoy a quiet drink and the beautiful, fragrant tree. About eleven o'clock the kids came down to join us. Geo shuffled around in front of the fireplace and Pam fiddled with some of the decorations on the tree. They were clearly uncomfortable. I had a moment of panic that they were upset about how close Cal and I had become and wanted to discuss it. I glanced at Cal but he gave me a sweet smile and turned to the kids, "Okay, what's with you two?"

Geo pulled up an ornate upholstered bench and they sat down together, facing us. He started, "Mom, we didn't know exactly how to go about this, but . . ." He opened his iPhone and scrolled down the menu and then handed it to me. "Read this, I got it yesterday. Cal already knows about it, I forwarded a copy to him yesterday."

Puzzled, I scanned the message. It was from Devon Wilkes, the attorney that had been working with George's attorney and had been helping us with the George mess. I quickly skimmed several pages and I handed the phone back to him. "Just give me the details, it would take me all night to digest all of this, I think I know what has happened, Cal? Geo?"

Geo cleared his throat. "Mom, I told you an untruth. After my last exam I flew to Florida to see Dad, and then Mr. Wilkes. I don't think Dad is going to claim me for quiet some time if ever. I really tore into him and asked him why he hadn't contacted Pam since he'd had the DNA test results in hand for almost two weeks. He started giving me a bunch of shit and said he was going to challenge it and that Pam had etc. etc. and poor Edison had just been taken in. I stood up and came really close to decking him . . . God; I almost physically attacked my own father. Anyway, long story short, I told him what he'd better do, and in the end, we set up a meeting with both our and his, actually Naomi's, attorneys. Naomi came along as did 'the coach.' In spite of his body muscular and beautiful, I came really close to taking him on. Naomi held me back and I came close to cracking her one or two as well. Anyway, it's all settled. Cal, can you explain the details, Mom and Pam need to know everything, and I probably won't get it straight."

I was astounded; my gentle, quiet son, who had adored his father, risked his own relationship to confront the wrong. I was speechless. From somewhere in the past I couldn't help but quoting, *to march in to hell for a heavenly cause.* I whispered, "Oh, Geo, my poor, dear boy!"

Cal took over, "We've been in constant communication ever since Geo let me know that he insisted on taking this route. I asked Pam's attorney, Mr. Abbot, if he would be jeopardizing Pam's lawsuits she intended to file. He said if we could keep it out of the courts it would be the best to bring it to a conclusion that otherwise could easily go on for years. So, we put our heads together and locked in the statuary rape scenario coupled with approximate prison time if convicted of that and related charges, factored in the destruction of his and Naomi's name and the press coverage that would drag her company into it, to say nothing of what George would have to stand up to and admit in court, and under oath."

I shook my head in amazement and motioned him to continue.

"I pulled in a couple of markers and had the engineering firm George and Naomi work for investigated and found out that she has controlling interest to the tune of 75% of the company, and that their annual billings are in the billions with clients all over the world. Our George has been doing quite a lot of traveling world-wide to work with some of the international clients. Also, Naomi owns multiple vacation resorts and rental units as well as some very favorable investments with Fortune 500 firms. To wit, the dame is loaded with her own earnings and properties, and she and the coach have inherited a bundle from dear old dad. So, Geo and I put together our strategy. Geo, bring us home."

Geo learned forward now carefully reading from his phone's documents, "Yeah, Dad's really in with this gal. He's invested deeply with her guidance and is pulling in a lot more than chicken feed, so with the assistance of our very astute Mr. Wilkes, this is the deal:

1st   "Sent to you by registered mail to Cal's office (Darcy said he'd be in the office working this week) will be the copies for Mom's signature of a no-fault divorce, to be finalized immediately. Interestingly, the original filing now almost over a year old was simple and clean in spite of the mocked up copy he sent to Father Mac for you to sign. Apparently the attorney pointed out many areas that they had incorporated into the simple no-fault original to frighten you could have been very strong opportunities for serious legal action on your part. I might say that Naomi's graphics staff can pretty well come up with anything she wants from notary stamps to forgery. You wouldn't have a chance against them, or at least it would take time and money you don't even need to think about any longer.

2nd   "Included in the package will be a fully legal notarized, witnessed and filed document relinquishing the biological father, Edison Coffman's, parental rights to the child he fathered, naming Pam the sole parent of the baby which means she can keep it freely or adopt it out without any future involvement from him.

3rd   "This one was a more difficult one since some properties had to be disposed of, Mom, you and Pam receive cashiers' checks in the amounts of $250,000 for you, and $500,000 for Pam, apparently amounts you had already suggested which they were very eager to supply.

4th   "Mom, you are now the owner of any and all communal assets you and Dad hold in Colorado or any other states. That means the house Darcy is buying is legally yours.

5th   "Here are all the therefores and herewiths: Pam will acknowledge Edison's compliance by signing the documents that will accompany the checks indicating she will not pursue any criminal charges against him nor will she publicize in any manner or in any press the circumstances of her relationship with him, nor will she or the child ever be in contact with him; sort of a permanent restraining order. Naomi said she must receive back her original copies of these notarized documents prior to Pam's cashing the check, which she has efficiently post-dated by three weeks. Furthermore, Pam will never attempt to obtain from Edison any further communications or compensations especially child support or further attempt to force or accept any contact with himself or his family by herself or the child. She agrees that the child will never know the name or area of residence of its biological father in spite of laws which may read to the contrary; he also wishes to hear no more, ever, regarding herself or the child, no matter what the circumstances.

<u>6th</u>   "Mom, you will agree to cease any and all attempts to personally contact George Joseph Brown except in the instance of an emergency with either of his children, George, Jr. or Pamela Brown. All communications shall be transmitted via respective attorneys, even in the event of an emergency, and all financial and divorce documents, duly signed and filed by both parties shall be determined to be final with no further action instigated by either and all named parties."

He looked up and smiled, "As I say, I don't think Dad is ever going to claim me. I came down pretty hard and once I had a grip, I didn't turn either of the three loose. Mr. Wilkes gave me so much material that what I didn't scream out, he calmly added. Even Naomi's great wealth and the seemingly death grip she has on Dad couldn't keep him from shaking in his boots. I hated every second of it, but nobody hurts my Mom or my baby sister.

"Mom, he tried to make me read what he called 'your demands,' at our first meeting when we were alone. Actually, that's where I got my figures, and both attorneys agreed to the amounts. Apparently they had already decided where to get the money to pay you off. It's hard to believe that that shit Edison was saved by his Mommy for such a high price tag, but I wanted to go for the juggler and so I did. This is a real hoot, though, Dad said he'd almost had it all figured out how he was going find a way to add his name to the list of those killed and missing in the 911 bombing of the World Trade Center Towers. He had taken steps to cash out his largest insurance policy and then was going to change his identity so he wouldn't have to deal with any of us. Apparently, he just couldn't get it all lined up. Of course, he blamed it on your refusing to leave him alone so he wasn't ever able to get his mind wrapped around it to bring it to fruition."

For the next hour we cried, talked, raged, and finally calmed down enough to call it a night. Pam and I went upstairs first, leaving the guys to sip some Gentleman Jack and hopefully find some smug comfort in their combined efforts. Pam and I said goodnight in the hallway. When as I headed to my room she gave me a hug and whispered in my ear, "*Mom, Geo and I don't really care if you share a room with Cal, after all, we're all adults here.*"

Chapter Nine

▼

The down comforter was so warm I didn't want to crawl out of bed and put my feet on the cold floor. Clarissa had installed a modern furnace and the old house stayed reasonably warm, but the walls weren't insulated and the floors were like ice. I would have stayed snuggled in but remembered that it was Christmas morning. In days gone by, the kids would have had be out of bed at the break of dawn to check on Santa . . . but, like the fleeting passage of time, they had moved into adulthood and would sleep until noon.

The faint aromatic tease of fresh coffee drifted up the stairs and that was more than enough to pull me out of my lethargic musings. I pulled on my heavy fleece robe and slippers, padded downstairs, and followed my nose into the kitchen. With mug in hand, the sound of crackling logs led me to the old sitting room on the far side of the house. Cal was perched on the ornate loveseat with his eyes intent on his laptop computer. The Christmas tree lights were glowing in the early morning darkness and the fireplace invited me to join him. I planted a quick kiss on his forehead, "No rest for the wicked, Santa?"

He smiled, "they tell me Satan never sleeps and I try to keep ahead of him. Actually, I brought along a few electronics and I've been finalizing the secure Wi-Fi network the office in DC established for me. Perfect connection, it's a strong signal and clear as a bell. We can reach anyone in the world, maybe even the universe from here."

I frowned, "Are you going to be able to take any time off at all? You're supposed to be on a holiday, you know."

He logged off and closed the laptop, "I am on holiday. Actually, I don't start in full time until the first of the year. I hope we'll stay here that long. I just need to finish up some paperwork for filing before then. I'll tell you more about it later, no big deal, really. I'm an independent contractor for the

Department of Homeland Security, so I have a bit of flex with how I handle my assignments. Don't look that way, there's scarcely any travel involved, work from home office mostly, and get paid by direct deposit . . . plus, absolutely minimal danger involved, any more questions?" He winked. The boy could read my mind.

While Cal put away his toys upstairs, I pulled the ottoman up in front of the comfortable Queen Anne chair I had placed next to the fireplace and rested my feet. Before I knew it, I had nodded off. I rarely allow myself to completely 'stay in the moment,' but it was impossible not to do so in this wonderful, cozy old house. It was several hours later when I started awake to the sound my two large children stomping down the stairs and landing in front of the tree. Just like old times. After plowing through gift wrap, discarded boxed, and piles of gifts we all jumped in and prepared a casual breakfast. Then everyone went back to bed for a long winter's nap . . . just like old times.

Benny and Gracie let themselves in and quietly went about preparing our Christmas dinner. They insisted that would be their gift to us. They refused to join us, only saying that all would be ready whenever we were. By two o'clock we were back downstairs, and going with the order of the day, wore warm slacks, sweaters, and bedroom slippers. Refreshed and happy, we tucked into a wonderful old-fashioned Christmas feast. I was so overcome with thankfulness and happiness that the trauma of the past few years simply melted away and dropped from my shoulders and my mind, or so I thought. Looking at my little family, I felt we had all passed through the fire and life would be happy again.

After a combined effort of clean-up and the securing of leftovers, Pam and Geo jumped on the new video games and the loud challenges soon filled the air. Cal land I bundled up and went for a quiet walk.

The sun was almost blinding as it glanced off the snow. After a while we stopped to rest on a large dry and warm flat rock and gave ourselves in to the silence and healing rays. We listened to the birds flitting about in the trees and Cal gently nudged me to see the four beautiful deer that were slowly making their way to the bit of trickling brook that had not frozen over. I remembered that I sent a lot of silent prayers heavenward that afternoon. How could God continue to bless me so!

He roused me out of my Zen-State by asking, "You haven't said anything about Father Mac since I got back. How's he doing?"

I was taken out of my emotional moments of solitude and shook my head, "The Chancery office managed to post bail and release him to a warden of some kind, and they immediately whisked him away. That new Polish priest took over completely at church, poor kid. The deacons were lined up to help him through all of the Christmas Masses and Children's programs. Mac was devastated but grateful. He called me once; they have him sequestered somewhere. He said he was definitely retiring after this murder mess. Somehow, after the first few stories, the papers have not been doing the big paparazzi thing. I suspect the powers at the top have pulled in some markers. Since it wasn't any salacious scandal, maybe it wasn't a top priority with the press, anyway. Now, can you fill me in on this new venture of yours?"

The deer now gone, he tossed a few pebbles into the stream, "You already know most of it. Way back then when I was in New York, I worked with a guy, an old friend, who must remain nameless, on a case that turned into an international incident. It went on and on, deeper and deeper until I was approached that it would be advisable for me to be thoroughly vetted and get a top secret security clearance so I could continue on the case. It took a long time. When I finally had my clearance, this incident had become a serious threat for several countries. I told you that I had killed a man, and it was in conjunction with this situation that it happened.

"My private cases were not nearly so intense, but, I was young and fancied myself another 007 type, you know, James Bond and all. I had loved the intrigue. So I kept my finger on the pulse and made myself available and from time to time my friend would bring me in on something.

"Well, he is retiring and contacted me to take up a section of some of the newer electronic identification operations, you know, eye, skeletal, etc. recognition. I want to tell you more but until we get you an administrative type clearance, I can't. You will basically fall under my supervision and classification since my status will be as a private contractor, but you'll have to get through the process on your own merits, which I'll help you with. I don't see any problems. I'll need you to be involved in a lot of the paperwork/reporting and possibly tracking, so I want us to get started as soon as possible. We can get your application documents sent to us here. Actually, I would like this to be our home base . . . Mosscreek, that is."

I was startled, "Here? Mosscreek? You mean travel back and forth from the condos daily?"

He cleared his throat, "No, I want us to get rid of the condos and move here, permanently."

"Cal, how we can possibly do that, I mean . . . ." He put his finger on my lips and dug into his jacket.

He opened a jeweler's box containing the most beautiful Marquise cut diamond I've ever seen in my life. "Like this. I want us to start this new life together. You're free now, and I want to grab you before the word gets out . . . Marry me, Middy, next week, as soon as your paperwork from Florida is filed.

I've been dying for years to ask you such a simple question . . . suddenly, I'm afraid of your answer." He took my hand and kissed me. "Will you?"

Suddenly, the cancer thing slammed me in the chest and I could hardly breathe. I was shaking so badly that he took my arms to steady me, I stammered, "I can't Cal, I love you desperately, but you should know I can't marry you, not now, not anymore."

His face clouded, "Why, in God's name Middy, Why?"

I pushed the tears off my face with my gloved right hand, "You don't understand, I've dreaded this minute, I've known it was coming and I know what I have to say, I can't Cal, it's the cancer. I'm not the same as I was when we . . . . you know, before. I have scars up both sides of my back from a part of the breast reconstruction process. Yes, I have two bumps on my chest that make me look normal, but it's not the same, only part of it is mine. I can't have you expecting that I'm a complete, whole woman, I'm not, I'm not!"

I slid off the rock and tried to walk away. He put his arms around me and turned me to face him. He'd unzipped his jacket and pulled up his sweater, "Look, I'm not whole. He pulled off my glove and took my hand. He traced my finger along a web of scars, "Open heart surgery, I can drop my slacks and show you the scars down my thigh if you'd like; I'm not the man I once was. Does it matter to you?"

I shook my head violently. He pulled down his sweater, "Middy, you silly girl. Why in the world should what's happened to us in this lifetime have any control over us and not allow us to go forward? I wanted to be with you during your surgery but I respected your privacy even though it nearly killed me. Your concerns are as unfounded now and they were then. Who sat by my hospital bed when I was shot and had that massive coronary? Did my resulting body scarring bother you then?"

I shook my head. He held up the ring and sadly placed it back in the pocket of his jacket. In that brief moment the sun captured it, splashing prismatic mementos around the landscape, "Middy . . . sit down. I really messed this up. I want you to understand that it's not Mosscreek, or you helping me with the new venture, or even any part of the George mess. I love you and won't ever let you get away. I don't honestly even know how long I've been in love with you; maybe even before I met you, I don't know. Don't say no to me, it would kill both of us. God, you survived and I've survived our life's medical crises . . . so far. Let's help one another from here on out. I'm so tired of being alone and longing to have you with me. Let's go on from here together, no matter what happens, I'll always love you but you can't deny me, Middy, you have to marry me, there's simply no other option!"

Against my better judgment, and through tears, I slipped my hand into his jacket pocket, took out the ring, and handed it to him. I gave him my left hand, "At least, let's see if it fits, apparently I'm not to ever lose it." I leaned into him and kissed him like I wanted it to last forever . . . as I prayed fervently that it would.

✳   ✳   ✳   ✳

Back at the house we found the kids in the kitchen stripping off turkey for sandwiches and piling their plates with leftovers, including the pumpkin pie and whipped cream. Apparently they'd gone through a full bag of potato chips while playing their games but it hadn't slowed down their youthful appetites. Cal and I grabbed plates and followed them back through the hall and we all found places by the fireplace. Geo added logs, and Pam looked like my little girl again, innocent, happy, and healthy. I sensed family talk session coming on. Cal cleared his throat and took my hand. He was suddenly uncomfortable.

"Geo, Pam, I really should have discussed this with you before now, but, well, I didn't trust your mother." He held up my hand which seemed to be much too small for the size of the ring on my finger. Pam squealed and crawled over to see it. She had been sitting on the floor next to her brother. Geo quickly swallowed whatever he had in his mouth and quickly washed it down with a slug of milk. He burst out laughing, wiping the spattering of lunch off his face.

Cal continued, "I suppose it's not a surprise that I've been crazy about your unpredictable mother for a long, long time, in fact much longer that it has been appropriate. I knew she'd probably refuse me today, but I lashed her to a tall aspen with woven rush fronds and she finally agreed to marry me. I guess now is the time for each of you to speak now or forever hold your peace, or whatever they say."

Geo cleared his throat, 'No, we get to do that at the wedding. Seriously, Congratulations. I really am happy that this is finally going to happen. I hate to admit it, but Mom's been through hell with our dad. I don't know what has happened to him, but it's been coming on for a long time. Mom, Pam and I both are happy for you. We want you to know that we're with you, and neither of us is even sure at this point how Dad's even going to fit in our lives, or if we want him to, or even if he wants to. Just please, you and Cal be happy. We're a family."

After all the hugs and tears and excitement, we settled down into the inevitable 'what's next' agenda. I started, "First of all, I want you both to know that Cal and I are both, individually and collectively financially self-sufficient.

God has blessed me with some surreal experiences, this beautiful house and grounds being one of the most unbelievable gifts. As soon as your father hooked up with Naomi, I had my attorney put this house, grounds, and any holdings into a trust for you two. I didn't want them to ever get their hooks on something that I wanted for you to have after I'm gone."

They looked at one another and held hands. Pam eyes became red and a tear trickled down. "Next of all, Cal and I have been here a couple of times and we've done some remodeling and updating. He has invested a lot of his own time and resources into Mosscreek with no strings attached; as you know he is painfully generous. This brings me to the second point. We would like to close out our condos and move here permanently. We've often thought of having a small resort offering for select clientele, which we may or may not pursue. Right now that's on the back burner."

Pam interjected, "Fine, but when is the wedding?"

Cal laughed, "I'll need your help getting her to the altar and she's being very evasive."

I smiled, "soon, we have a lot of details to sort our, but I promise, as soon as possible."

Cal took his turn, "We talked a bit about the condos on the way back to the house. It seems that the woman who owns the condo your mom has been leasing wishes to sell it. She's written that she's married a very successful photographer, like herself, and they have lodgings all over the world and travel almost constantly. She has offered to sell her condo to your mother. Now, I have a condo and was fortunate enough to be able to pay cash for it since I'd closed out my house in Long Island. This is a suggestion we wanted to put to the two of you."

I took over. "Pam, I know that you will be staying at Samantha and Dan's house a great deal of the time. While you were in the hospital, she told me that she hoped you'd be in favor of certain limited hours throughout the week to care for the children. She said you could have your own quarters in the rooms over the garage that was the mother-in-law suite. They've offered to let you live there full time whether you're on duty or not. Sam wants to be a hands-on mother, but would like to have some time for her activities. They do expect you to continue college and they will work around your classes each semester so you have ample time to do your studies. Dan also said that in their extreme gratitude, all your expenses, tuitions, plus a stipend would be paid, and he is buying you a car so you don't feel like you are stranded."

Pam solemnly nodded. Geo looked at her and tried to read her feelings. She then smiled. "Everyone, I've wanted to tell you all this for a long time, but I am going to be fine taking care of little Jason and baby Victoria. All the time I was pregnant, I was praying for God to give me the right family for my baby. I didn't know if it was going to be a boy or a girl but it didn't matter. From the time Sam and Dan and I came to our agreement, I started talking to my unborn baby. I told it about its new family, what they liked, where they lived, about Jason's toys he would be sharing, and what a sweet mommy and daddy it would be getting. I used to put my iPod earphones on my stomach and play the music Sam liked. Sometimes, I think the baby danced. Anyway, I never thought of the baby as mine. I want you all to know that Victoria belongs to Sam, Dan, and Jason. I'm happy to be a part-time nanny. For a long time I was horrified that I'd never be able to finish college and wouldn't find someone that I trusted with a new baby, in that case, I'd have to be a single mom and that didn't even merit thinking about. God took care of all of that. I can't believe all that they will be doing for me. Cal, you have a wonderful family, and now we are a family together." She got up and gave him a big hug and sat down next to me and put her head on my shoulder.

We sat in silence for a long time. Geo got up and fiddled with the logs in the fireplace, Cal left us alone and went into the kitchen and made a new pot of coffee. I patted the space next to me and Geo sat down. "Is this all right with both of you? You've been through so much. I don't want to make things uncomfortable for you, or make you unhappy. You know my feelings and love for you are off the charts. Nothing could make me more proud of what you've both done with your lives; Geo, having the courage to go and face your father and negotiate the settlement of this dreadful divorce, and Pam, handling the crime that was committed against you with such maturity. I want you to be honest with me . . . what are your concerns? Please be honest."

Geo spoke up, "Dad, that's my concern. I want him to leave you and us the hell alone. I read that jacked up divorce document he and Naomi sent to Father Mac for you to sign. I really hated him. The attorney almost wouldn't let me see him in person, I was almost violent. I honestly don't care if Pam or I ever see him again. That Naomi is a bitch on wheels. She's too powerful to ever get involved with. I'm scared for all of us that she might retaliate if we cross her."

Pam nodded, "She has a very sick attachment to that creep Edison and to Dad. He can hardly do anything that she hasn't orchestrated. You can bet Dad didn't organize the settlement. Geo laid down the law and I'm sure Dad went whimpering to her. I'm not going to pursue anything with Edison. The baby is safe and I'm signing all the papers to get him out of our lives. He'll never know where she is. And, we're all taking those checks and depositing them. I'm not going to let my anger ruin my life. I had a hard enough time staying calm so I wouldn't disrupt my pregnancy. I agree with Geo. I want them to leave us alone. They, all three, are dangerous. Let's make darn sure that those documents don't have any loop holes and the checks are good."

I interjected, "And my marrying Cal? Moving here? Are you both okay with that . . . please be honest?"

Cal knocked on the door frame, "Can the culprit come back in?"

We all laughed, Pam ran to him and grabbed his hand, "Get in here step-father." She made a fist when he sat down where she had been and held it in his face, "You get to meet dese five mafia dudes right in the nose if you ain't nice to da lady."

He grabbed her fist and kissed it, "Yep, you're as feisty as your mom. I can see where my challenges lie! Can we get to the condo issue?"

I shrugged, "As Cal said, my condo will be going up for sale. We were thinking that maybe the two of you might want a *pied-à-terre* in Denver. A place where you would have a residence and a place we could stay when we want to spend time in town. We have a couple of options. I could buy my condo and you could split the payments, which are pretty low and I think you could manage, that way you'd both own it. Cal and I could keep his and have it for our in town residence. Or, we could just give up mine and we'd keep Cal's and you would have the guest room to share. Pam, I'm sure you'd like to get away on your own from time to time."

Geo spoke up, "From my vantage point, I'm going to take that year abroad in *Riyadh* and work for an engineering firm. Don't plan on putting together any permanent residence for me. Who knows where I'll end up? I'm really excited about it, as you all know."

Pam shrugged, "I don't know, maybe if you just kept Cal's place, I could have the guest room if I want to get away anytime. I don't really want the responsibility of a place of my own while I'm in school, I think I'd be spread too thin. I want to do my best in school and hopefully go to grad school, maybe back East. By then Jason and Victoria will be in playschool and they won't need me."

Cal smiled, "Well, that's okay by me, what do you think wife to be, when do we marry and move?"

I laughed, "Let's see what comes in the mail next week, then we'll make a collective decision."

Geo cleared his throat, "I hate to be the party pooper, but I'd like to get back to Mom's condo and pick up some things and get back to Boulder. Some of the guys and I have planned a skiing trip, if that's all right with you, Mom."

Pam jumped in, "And, if it's okay, I told Sam I'd be there by the end of the week. If I could use your car for a while, Mom, I'd like to go back, too Geo."

I sighed, "Well, it was nice while it lasted, but of course I know you both have things you need to do. I'm just happy that we've had this time together. Cal and I have to do some serious planning if we are going to make this his base of covert activities."

And then he had to explain his new job while I went back to the kitchen and cleaned up.

CHAPTER TEN

▼

The tenth of January came far too soon. It found me back in my condo, Cal back at the office, and Geo and Pam doing whatever it was that they had decided to do. I must report, however, that New Year's Eve found us all gathered at Samantha and Daniel's home for an early dinner and to officially meet little Victoria; and I suppose to formally welcome the Brown family into their family. I was rather embarrassed at the elaborate fuss over my extravagant diamond, but Cal assured all that he wanted it to be up front and visible so everyone would know I had finally said the magic word. The date and place of the upcoming nuptials were still undecided.

It was odd to admit that I had no maternal, or rather grandmotherly maternal feelings for little Victoria. Seeing her with Pam did not pull at my heartstrings and that surprised me. I think Pam's conviction that the baby had always belonged to Sam had already taken hold on all of us, and because she was going to be my step-granddaughter, I was sure that other sort of warmth I felt when I held her was quite acceptable. I was happy with the comfortable knowledge that God was in His Heaven and all seemed to finally be right on Earth.

The paperwork from George and Naomi came through as stated. Pam, Geo and I met with our attorneys, and we went through everything line for line. We had taken the cashier's checks to the bank and had them verified. They were good and available January tenth. Both attorneys indicated that in spite of Naomi and George's post-dated cashing requirements, they insisted on negotiating an agreement with them that would allow us to have the money in hand and then simultaneously fax copies of the signed documents, to be of course express mailed and hand-delivered after the fact. They both shook their heads at the restrictive language inserted into our agreements, stating that any good attorney could walk all over it in court. But, we were happy to sign and get the matter closed. I asked my attorney to take care of the details of changing the ownership of the mortgage on my house. I wouldn't see any benefit for a long time, but it made me happy to be able to know Darcy and I would work out any problems or needs with the lease without George's constant whining and interference.

Maybe I forgot to mention it, but when George left me I didn't want to stay in the house. Our dear Officer, office assistant and friend, Darcy and his wife agreed to sell their darling little house to me and I worked out an arrangement with George that allowed Darcy to buy our house with very generous terms on all sides. Unfortunately, after an incident with one of my Mother's 'friends' I was very uncomfortable about living alone in Darcy's house. So, I put it on the market and leased my completely secure condo.

At long last, it was a very strange feeling to be actually legally free of George. I gave Geo a portion of my cash. He refused it at first but without his actions who knows how long this would have gone on. He agreed to accept it when I pointed out that I wanted his time in *Riyadh* to be free from financial worries. He assured me that his salary was going to be far, far above what any firm in the U.S. would pay him, but he smiled and said that I'd made it possible for him to have enough money to court the dark-eyed daughter of a sheikh if he so desired. I let that matter drop!

Pam was anxious to move forward with the adoption documents and work with the financial advisor her attorney recommended to protect her cash settlement. Mr. Abbot, the attorney, told her that he wasn't quite comfortable letting Naomi's son off the hook for the serious crime he committed and said if he dug deeply enough, he might find out that it wasn't completely legal for him to do so. Pam begged him to drop it since it could interfere with the baby's future. Reluctantly, he agreed. I suspect though, as ethical as he'd always been, he'd checked it out anyway just for his own edification.

∗   ∗   ∗   ∗

Cal had been pressuring me about setting the date and I just didn't know what to do. He was deep into his work and needed to get moved to Mosscreek and install the new equipment that the Department of Homeland Security was ready to deliver to him. I had to do so something about my condo and had yet to contact Ms. Prentiss, the owner, even though she'd left the timeline pretty open. My house, the Darcy house, finally sold, the cash in hand was less than I'd hoped for especially after the sales commission had been deducted, but at last it was over. Now there was the question of all my furniture and so many decisions to make that I just kept procrastinating. I had all my DHS (Dept of Homeland Security) security clearance paperwork notarized and mailed, but had yet to take a polygraph test and could only hope that my references and personal interviews would prove to the powers that be that I was respectable and qualified to keep deep dark secrets. I think Cal and the guys at the top had made an agreement to put my paperwork on a fast-track. He never ceased to amaze me.

I was at my computer typing up a list of "to dos" when my e-mail beeped. A message from Cal:

> *Notice: Nuptials for Madge "Middy" M. Brown and Calvin C. Cleere scheduled for February 14, Valentine's Day, in the chambers of Judge Judith Westwood, City Hall, Denver, Colorado. 3:00 PM. Reception to follow at the Brown Palace Hotel, Denver, Colorado—RSVP*

What to do? I just didn't know if I was ready to move forward. I still had so much baggage. My mind skidded over the past. George and I had eloped, in other words, we came together without benefit of clergy so I know all of those years, I really wasn't a good Catholic since my marriage hadn't been sanctioned by the Church. But time passed quickly. Both sets of parents were surprised and distressed at our obstinate behavior since they hoped for the huge wedding/reception thing with a cast of thousands, but we hadn't cared. As time passed, though, we still went to church regularly, got involved in all sorts of activities, raised our kids as proper Catholics, and as far as we were concerned, it was no one's business but our own. Way down deep, I certainly hadn't wanted to remarry George in any 'official" church ceremony. I thought the idea was ridiculous. We had two kids and a marriage license, which was certainly enough to yoke us together.

Cal and I had discussed the time and place often enough and I just couldn't commit. I hoped a marriage in a judges' chamber would turn out much better than the last quickie in a registrar's office. For the past weeks I had hoped it would be on the grounds of Mosscreek, maybe by the little stream under a gazebo . . . but, it was winter and I knew Cal wouldn't wait till the flowers bloomed and the songbirds took flight. *So, what else could I do but RSVP?* I just hadn't been able to move forward and he knew how to take matters a step further. Suddenly, I smiled and was surprised at how excited I'd become.

My fingers began tapping away on the keyboard to itemize my rapidly growing list. It looked like I'd have just under a month to get everything done. Probably we'd get Cal, at least, moved to Mosscreek so he could get his business computers and electronics installed. I hoped to be able to refrain from being involved in all of those decisions. We'd already refurbished the large bedroom, bath, and sitting room near the end of the long hallway upstairs as our master area; we just had to decide on which furnishings to use. The room at the very back of the hall and next to the master would be Cal's office since the view out of the window was spectacular, afforded the most privacy, and would be easy to secure. We'd begun some construction with new stud walls filled with insulation and were waiting for the contractor to come in and put up drywall, finish soundproofing walls, floors, ceiling, and ready the room for all the new electrical outlets. The electrician had to install a much larger panel to take care of his requirements and all of our power hungry extravagances, but Cal said all was going well.

How could I help but keep smiling as I reached for my ringing cell phone and answered with a cheery "hello."

Chapter Eleven

▼

A strangled voice greeted me, *"Madge, is that you? Madge . . ."*

"Father Mac? This is Madge, are you all right?"

"I have to see you now, Madge, can you come right away. I'm desperate, please."

I glanced at the clock, "Mac, what is it, are you injured? Where are you?"

He whispered, *"I'm in a house near the seminary, hurry, I can only get away for a few minutes, I'll be waiting for you"*

He quickly gave me the directions and I jotted them down as I ran for my coat. Lord, what was going on now?

I decided to take I-25 and then the Broadway exit. In record time I pulled up in front of a cozy little house with well maintained grounds and a clean shoveled walkway. Mac came rushing down the drive and practically took an Olympian dive into the front seat. He ducked down and whispered breathlessly, *"Back out quick, turn at the corner and cross over Colorado Boulevard. There's a fast food something or other on the right. Pull in."*

I let him catch his breath as I pulled in and ordered two coffees on the drive-through mic. Then I pulled around to the parking lot and turned off the motor. "Okay, what's going on?"

He took a gulp of his coffee before answering; finally in a somewhat normal voice his words came rushing out, "I'm under some sort of an honorary house arrest. The Brother who lives at the house is at a funeral this afternoon and I am supposed to stay put, but Madge, I have no one I can trust, please help me. That Johnny fellow, he's set me up."

I looked up toward Heaven needing patience and understanding, "Mac, slow down, how did he set you up. I'd hoped by now that your attorney would have had it all sorted out. What's happened?"

He grabbed my arm, "He passed a polygraph test, you know a lie detector test. They said he's telling the truth. My attorney is putting pressure on me to see how we can discredit him *if* I'm telling the truth. Johnny gave a statement and signed it, he said that I told him in Confession to kill that Mahoney woman because I didn't know how else to deal with her. Middy, he said I told him in *Confession* to kill her, so he did, kill her, he did!"

It took a full minute before it all penetrated my tired skull. During that time I did a quick replay of the taped facts I'd stored away in my mind over a month ago. *Mac an accessory after the fact, Murder One for Johnny DeBeers, handyman at the church, crazy Mary Magdalene worshiper at church with a broken neck dead in the snow on church grounds, ensuing arrest and incarceration of Johnny, no bail set, Father Mac, posted bail, moved to a safe house near the Seminary by Diocesan or Diocesan-recommended attorney, relieved of all priestly duties.* I clicked back to the present, "Okay, I remember the facts. Can't you just take your own polygraph test to prove you are telling the truth? I'm practically positive that you didn't even so much as imply such a course of action to Johnny . . . right?"

He was almost in tears by now, "That's just it; they won't let me take a lie detector test!"

"Mac, who and why?"

"Who? Everybody, my attorney and everybody at the Chancery office or the Bishop, or whoever is overseeing this mess; maybe even the Vatican . . . I don't know except that it is not permitted for a priest to undergo any type of questioning that might involve the sacred bond of the Confessional. So, that means that I can't tell them what I didn't say or what I did say that he could have misconstrued, and now I can't prove what the truth really is! I'm a dead duck!"

After a deep breath and a sip of coffee, I asked the question that was beginning to sink me into the inevitable quicksand that Cal was always warning me about, "What can I do to help Mac since I have no power whatsoever over the Vatican?" I said it in sort of a sassy manner, but good Lord, what was Mac thinking?

He took my arm again and glanced around like we were being recorded, "Go see Johnny. Work it out of him, why is he lying? What did I ever do that he is involving me like this, and Madge, you have to work fast, my sister insists on coming to get to the bottom of this, and you've met her . . . she'll involve the Holy Father even if she has to go to Rome personally and shake his shoulders till his teeth rattle, she'll ruin me! They'll excommunicate me even before I go to prison, Dear God, I'm doomed. I'd kill myself right now if I wasn't certain it would send me directly to hell without passing Go or collecting $200.00, or if my sister could come after me and yank me back to face the music!"

After our covert encounter, the end of which had me park down the street a few houses and watch the stealth scurrying of my dear friend as he looked like the spy who came in from the cold. I waited until he had given me the okay sign and closed the door before I made a U-turn and went back up Colorado Boulevard. I had the very crazy idea that I should erase the last hour, turn around again and just go to Park Meadows Shopping Center and start looking for a wedding dress. Maybe this had all just been a dream . . . a nightmare . . . *right!*

✱   ✱   ✱   ✱

As the best laid plans often turn sour, we couldn't close the P.I. business as hoped on the first of January. Several pending cases popped up and Cal did a double duty for a while to keep the status quo going. We decided to keep Darcy on till the first of February at least, and told him we were both retiring to the country. He took it well. He'd earned a nice promotion at the Precinct and was in a much better financial position than he'd been in a long time. Evelyn, his beautiful wife, had started an online business of designing and making precious children's clothing, and now that she had our old big house to work in, Darcy smilingly complained that her stuff was spread out all over the place. He was proud of her and said she was making a lot more than her own pocket money. I made a promise to visit her. Now that I was going to be a grandmother, I could shop for babies. I'd long neglected too many people.

Anyway, I still had Police Sergeant Darcy Davenport as my direct information center. I drove to the office. I trotted in with the excess energy-driven frustration I was trying to keep at bay with a big smile, "Hey Darcy, what's going on today? Cal out?"

"He is, boss lady, but if you want to wait, he's due back soon. He's out at your country place, had to meet some people he said. What you doing here? Ain't you supposed to be out shopping for your big day?"

I plopped my jacket on the coat rack, "Oh, I haven't really grabbed onto the fact yet that I have to. It's going to be a very small affair so no hurry. Pam and I have to get dresses and Cal is buying the flowers. What could be less urgent than that?"

He leaned back in the office chair while I wandered aimlessly around the room. Darcy smiled, "Evelyn and I are really happy to be included with the list of guests. Are you still sure you don't want us to throw a nice party before the event of the season?"

I carried a wilted plant to the sink and turned on the water, "Thank you but no. I love you both but that house holds too many scary memories. I think we'll all be fine to just gather at Sam's the evening before and drink champagne till the wee hours. Cal and I love you for the offer, though. Once I finish putting my past behind me, we'll come often and bother you for more summer barbeques."

He motioned to the chair in front of the desk, "You're making me nervous; sit down so we can visit." I returned the plant to the window sill and sat down, drying my hands on a paper towel. "So, how are the kids? Evelyn? Did Santa bring them everything they wanted?"

He laughed, "And more. Most of those electronic gadgets are out of batteries or broken. Anyway, where have you been keeping yourself? Cal said he was trying to make you take some time off so you can see what retirement's going to feel like. As for me, I can't imagine somebody as antsy as you are sitting still for more that five minutes. So, what brings you here to see old Darcy?"

I smiled my sweetest and most innocent smile, "Oh, nothing much. I just missed being here; I really loved all the time we've spent together, that's all."

He studied me for a minute; a frown took the place of his usual big happy smile, his eyes locked on mine before he looked up at the ceiling twirling a pencil, after a while he sighed, "Hummm. Hummmm. Well, you know, a while back I was down at the Precinct reading up on some of the open cases and I started scratching my head. I said to myself, 'Sergeant Davenport' I really like the sound of that, you know my new promotion, anyways I said to myself, '*Sergeant Davenport,* what's that little something that's niggling in the back of your mind?'

"For a spell I just couldn't put my finger on it. Seems as though there was a murder, some poor church woman got her neck broke and was left lying in the snow at the very church where our own boss lady has been known to attend. Further more, that same poor old priest that once took this same boss lady for a ride on his big Harley Davidson motorcycle, the one that was somehow involved in a wreck that killed some nun impersonator that had right before that, kidnapped that boss lady. As I recall reading on that case report, I'm positive that same priest with the Harley had just been arrested for being involved in the murder of this church lady, the one with the broke neck. And after a while, still scratching my head, I say to myself again, '*Sergeant Davenport, now how can this be? No place in that entire report did I see the name of our own Missy Brown, the same afore mentioned boss lady?*'

He glanced at me before continuing, "Then I wondered how that could *possibly* be, seeming as how she and that old priest been friends since long before I come to know her. Hummmm?' Missy Brown, can you clear up my mind on that? It just don't seem natural to me, does it to you? Now I know in the past the head boss of this here *CC Investigations* has got his drawers in a knot when one of his staff has got *herself* into a pickle or two should we say, and that niggling little thing in the back of my mind makes me wonder if that same Missy Brown might be trying to work undercover, and if so, she must know that is a *real bad* idea."

I leaned forward, "Damn it, Darcy. Can't this be just between the two of us? I need some help. Father Mac is desperate, he can't defend himself. He's begging me to help him. How can I say no to such a dear old friend?"

He tossed his pencil across the room and it landed perfectly into one of the coffee mugs by the sink, he muttered, "ten points for the sergeant." He walked across the room and retrieved his pencil then pulled the office chair over to in front of the desk where he could lean directly into my face. "Understand? Ten points for the sergeant, I had you figured out from the very first. I know you inside and out young lady, and I knew straight from day one we were bound to be having this discussion. I am not going to be a part of this. Cal is trying to retire, I got new responsibilities, and you might just be in well over your head. I'm only working here for a few more weeks and what you're thinking about is gonna go on for a long, long time. You can't involve me now or when I'm at the station and I'd like you to think about giving our poor boss a break this time. I love you, Sweetheart, but your friend has got an attorney. The whole Catholic organization ain't gonna let him fry without a solid case and furthermore, Cal is gonna kill you dead before the wedding if he gets wind of what you're probably thinking of doing. In fact, I was gonna leave you just a few minutes ago and ask you to close up the office so I can head downtown to pick up a few things before my shift. But now we both gonna plant our butts right where they are and when Cal comes in, I'm gonna sit here and smile like a Cheshire cat while you tell him what you're going to do. By the way, what is it, just for the record?"

I was what I felt, justifiably indignant, "I just want to know how I can get in to see the handyman and ask him some questions. He's lied to implicate Father Mac and the problem is that he passed his polygraph test. He said, under oath, that when he was in the Confessional, Father Mac told him to kill the woman. Of course that's a lie. Father Mac wants to take the polygraph to prove it but the Church won't let him because it would violate the bond of the Confessional and he can't tell anyone what he did or did not say. He has no one to turn to. I have to help him. How do I get in to see this Johnny guy?"

He gave me a smug smile, "He's got his self slapped with Murder One at his arraignment with no bail. I'd say they think he is a pretty serious criminal. Bottom line, probably nobody can see him except his attorney, who ain't going to want you meddling; and his priest . . . maybe Father Mac can do the snooping himself . . . no wait, he's an accessory."

He reached out and took my hand, "Middy Brown, don't get involved in this. Your priest is asking too much of you. You are on the very verge of ruining your relationship with Cal. He loves you, he needs to trust you. I'd want to skin Evelyn alive if she tried to pull something this dangerous behind my back, and she is the love of my life. A husband can only be expected to endure so many turns of the screw and come out smiling. For both your sakes, don't pursue talking to this guy, you're getting involved in a murder. He killed a woman in cold blood. You know nothing about him. Walk away."

I tried to make him understand, "I can't. I won't go behind anyone's back, a least not Cal's or yours, but Mac has no one who is close enough to him, who knows him well enough to believe in him. He's old and to most people, senile. They've brought in a young new priest and he is full of energy, has fresh new ideas, and has in less than a month turned the entire congregation around. Mac's fifteen minutes of fame, *the murder*, have come and gone. They've packed up his office and put his things in storage. He's living in a safe house to keep him out of the public eye until the trial. Do you actually believe anyone gives a damn about what happens to him?"

"What happens to whom?" Cal had opened the door and caught just the end of my anguished discourse.

I smiled and casually made a *no big deal* gesture with my hand, "Father Mac. I need to help him someway, Cal, and hope someone can come up with some ideas. His case is really complicated."

I could read the expression on his face and knew immediately that Darcy had given him the *here we go again* look. Cal took off his jacket and hung it on the hook next to mine. I could tell he was tired. His boots and jeans were splattered with sheetrock texture and good old Mosscreek mud. I didn't want to get into this whole thing now so I smiled. "It's nothing that can't wait. I'm open to suggestions, maybe the three of us can talk about it tomorrow"

Darcy said upon rising from the chair and moving it back to behind the desk, "I'm not in the office for the rest of the week. Cal's definitely the one who could come up with the right approach. Well folks, I'm off. See you next Monday."

He went to the sink and washed out his mug and took his jacket off the hook next to the one Cal had commandeered. I called out as he frowned at me behind Cal's back and then closed the door. I called out cheerfully, "Love to Evelyn and kids. Maybe we can do a pizza night soon." I had no choice but to drop the Father Mac thing . . . obviously this was not the time.

CHAPTER TWELVE

▼

January seemed to rush to a close and I hadn't yet drummed up the courage to talk to Cal about Father Mac. We spent every day at Mosscreek, painting, having carpeting installed, original old single pane windows replaced with new energy-efficient but style-appropriate ones, and our offices set up. I'd had the second of my security clearance interviews and didn't know if my references had yet been checked. I prayed that my prior situation with George wouldn't keep me from working with Cal, but all I could do was wait and hope. I hadn't done anything serious enough to be a matter of record but he could really mess me up. I wondered if he would lie under oath just to get back at me for some imagined wrong since I didn't even understand him anymore . . . or had I ever?

Cal had passed off my concerns saying I hadn't committed any criminal offence, been charged or arrested, and had proven my stability and had undergone training during the years of working in his office. After all, I had passed the concealed weapon vetting long ago and continued to stay current with my certificate and training.

My little pal, my .38 snub-nosed pistol was always with me since it had once been stolen. After that and the most severe dressing down I'd ever received from Cal, I got his message loud and clear. My little snub-nose had been stolen from my purse at a party and later turned out to be the murder weapon used by the party hostess to get rid of an of her ex-con husband. I'm really careful, extremely careful and always alert knowing what I'm responsible for. I go to the shooting range often. I receive the *Concealed Carry Report* and take every word very seriously. I've been a member of the *US Concealed Carry Association* from day one. I try not to dwell on the past even though I often think about how the brief years spent with Cal have changed me from dependable dull Madge the housewife to Middy, the . . . . ?? What? I'd have to think on that.

Cal and I were back at Mosscreek and had been sitting in the old drawing room situated directly under the rooms we were remodeling and at the far end of the downstairs when I came up with an idea. "What would you think of closing off this room and adding another staircase along this wall up into into the third bedroom next to ours? I'm thinking with the fireplace down here, we could make this our own sitting room and have the stairs open into our own private space, which would include the offices and master suite. We'd gain another bathroom and create one for each of us. We'll have different schedules, you're an early bird and I'm a night owl. We could then close off the rest of the upstairs hall at the right of the existing staircase." I scribbled up a sketch, "Here we could have access to the remaining six guest areas which would keep guests completely away from our part of the house . . . what do you think."

He took the sketch from me and made a few more scribbles and handed it back. He leaned over and pulled some cobwebs out of my hair and kissed me. "Genius! I'd been a bit concern about having strangers about and I know you still want to do your guest-weekend project. He ran his finger over his additions. 'With a nice solid door and a sturdy lock right here between the two staircases we'd be secure and out of the reach of any curious visitors. A new wall between the two stairs could be insulated for soundproofing. Actually, I should have thought about that more fully. We're a great pair . . . let me grab the twenty-five foot tape. I think the most important thing is to have the contractor match the existing stairway and doors in here so we can keep the character of the house." He started looking up at the ceiling and was already deep into the project. I was somewhat unsettled that whatever his involvement with The Department of Homeland Security might be, it seemed to be going forward as a top priority.

*   *   *   *

We were back having dinner in Cal's condo, mellowing out with our second bottle of wine when, finally two weeks after meeting with Father Mac, I broached the taboo subject. "Cal, can I bring you up to date on that visit I had with Father Mac?"

He motioned to our chairs in beside the fireplace and picked up the bottle of wine. He angled the chairs to face one another, topped off my wine, and we spent a few moments just enjoying the quiet and the warmth. It had begun snowing again and the lights from the parking area around the corner splashed over onto the large snowflakes drifting down at the edge of the golf course. I sighed and entered in to the long and anguishing discourse. I finished with, "How to you think I can possibly help, or if I can help?"

He refilled our glasses again and rubbed his eyes, "Oh, Middy, I want us out of this sort of involvement. I can understand you wanting to help him, but we're moving on. I don't want you put into another situation that has all the earmarks of an unhappy and possibly tragic ending. What course of action have you even imagined you could engage in that would help him? What if this handyman really believes that Father Mac encouraged him? The guy has already confessed to the murder, and he's being held without bond. At least the priest is in a safe house and out of the public eye. You don't need to be involved in a murder investigation. He has an attorney; can we please let the law take its course without us this time?"

I leaned forward, "But Cal, that day when you came into the office and I was talking to Darcy, I had just asked him if there was anyway I could visit with that Johnny guy in jail and see if I could maybe just pick up something. I don't know, maybe see if I could claim that none of the church staff knew where to find his records or keys and maybe I could make some sort of discovery about all this by just talking to him. He and Mac have been very close. It doesn't make sense. He was in charge of hiring and supervising all the repairs and things at church and he did have access to everything, or maybe I could just ask his attorney to pass on the message and evaluate what he would tell me. There has to be something we're missing. What could those Magdalene women possibly have done that would end in murder? Father Mac said that Johnny was a very good and spiritual man, a decorated military officer. He had to have had some serious provocation. I just have to do something no matter how small it is."

"Middy Darling, no; first of all, stay *completely* away from the accused. Father Mac is in a panic and your handyman is behind bars. That means they are hot Press fodder even if you don't see cameras hanging out behind the trees. You are in a precarious position with your security clearance. Everything you do can be recorded and taken into consideration. I know you love the old guy but your future, *our future together*, is far more important right now. I'm sorry to say that the most they'd give your friend is a prison sentence. Aren't priest retirement homes pretty much a prison-like environment anyway? There's always a chance they'll let him off. They have pretty flimsy case against him anyway if that Johnny's word is all they have. They'd have to drum up some better evidence that'll stick unless I miss my bet. He's an old guy, darling, and he has an attorney. Let it go, don't get involved unless something new comes up that involves *us* in the legal and official position within the operations of what's left of the fragments of *CC Investigations*."

"Oh Cal, that sounds so harsh! He has a sister who is trying to make him let her take over. She's been trying to get him to retire and move to Florida with her. Surely there's someway I can be instrumental in helping that come to fruition?"

He smiled, "With what he told you about his pushy sister, I'd think prison would be far more agreeable! Anyway, let's talk about what you think you can do, speak up, I'll try to be open-minded, but . . .

We ran over a few ideas, nothing too productive. I came away with the very firm warning that whatever I thought or planned to do about anything, *CC Investigations* was soon to be no more and there was no longer anyone called *Middy Brown, Assistant PI.* AND, to *stay completely away from and out of quicksand!*

I gave him a quick overview of my new idea about the situation and he grudgingly said I could do that and *no more* unless we discussed it further. Why did I come away feeling like a naughty five year old? Oh, well. I did care but I thought for certain my idea was a good one. I knew Cal had a lot on the line and I had the capability of becoming a security disaster that would ruin his entire future. It frightened me that he loved me enough to give me more than enough rope to hang both of us. Gads! What a mess! I wished fervently I could just close my mind to Mac's poignant plea for help. In fact, someway I had to, *but I'd really be careful!*

With Cal's less than encouraging blessing, the next day found me at the church. I'd made an appointment with the secretary and had only a very simple task; I wanted to peruse the scrapbook she kept with all of the obituary newspaper reports of our deceased parishioners. I remembered that the Mahoney woman's body had been shipped back East somewhere for burial, but that's about all I knew. I wanted to see all those mentioned in the remembrances. That was accomplished very easily. Apparently several people had also wanted to find relatives and loved ones of Mary Martha Mahoney with the intent of sending condolence messages. I made my list. Two sisters were also members of our parish, and the members of the Magdalenes' were all listed as loved by the deceased. That comprised quite a list and the names of some surprised me. The elderly parents lived in Pittsburg, Pennsylvania where she had been interred.

Next, still within Cal's safety zone allowances, I made a call to the middle sister, Mary Elizabeth Mahoney, who said she would be happy to meet with me, the younger sister, Mary Anne Mahoney, preferred to stay somewhat *cloistered.* Hummm . . . intrigue already.

The next quirky thing came about how and where she agreed to meet me. *I have some errands to run and I've taken off work on Friday. I'll be in South Denver at the new IKEA store just off I-25, near the Park Meadows Shopping center. Meet me for lunch in the cafeteria at 1:20. I love their Swedish Meatballs. I should be able to give you a half hour. I'll be wearing my good blue winter coat.*

Good blue winter coat? Was this to be an event? Well, I was certainly looking forward to Friday . . . What? A good Magdalene and Catholic woman would be ordering *meatballs* on Friday? Well, she was certainly modern. I expected some softly quiet nun-like piety given all the hype I'd heard about their loving gospel outreach, but she sounded extremely self assured and . . . bossy? It had been years since the general populous of we Catholics had been happily adhering to the meat-on-Friday-okay-except-during-Lent thing. Many of the more penitent, however, still observed some of the pre-Vatican II regulations.

Well, guess what. I did in fact recognize Mary Elizabeth Mahoney from having seen her in church. Since I fear I've kept a sinner's low profile, she didn't recognize me and thought I was a new parishioner excited about the latest salacious turn of events, i.e. the murder, and that I most likely was eager to join the Magdalene's.

Mary Elizabeth Mahoney carried a rather large tote bag and after the first two vigorous attacks on the meatballs, which were very good, she paused and began to pull out publications. She fanned them out on the table in front of us, "My dear, these are our pamphlets. We publish a monthly newsletter as well; I've added the last few copies. Of course with the horrible death of our leader, we've all been at loose ends, but don't let that keep you from seriously investigating a membership. I've been elected to continue the presidency after a two month mourning period. Until then, our meetings will be more a sharing of information, discussions, and that sort of spiritual fulfillment. Our international organization publishes a quarterly *Info-zine* and I've enclosed the last three. The next one will of course, feature Mary Martha and her research projects. There is so much work to be done. Now that that stupid old priest is gone we should be able to move forward quickly. The new young Father Pieter seems most willing to work with us. The old Deacons of course will always be a problem but we have plans to circumvent their interference."

At last I jumped in as she happily masticated, "I'm very intrigued with the events surrounding such a tragic event at the church. I believe your handyman has confessed to the murder? This must be so very difficult for your family, and of course, for the Magdalenes; what could have possibly led to such a tragedy, and wasn't the old priest involved? It just gives me the shivers!"

Boy was that ever the right thing to say! She put down her fork and leaned across the distance between us until we were almost nose to nose, "Oh, that pair. Poor Mary Martha had her hands full! That Johnny person, the handyman, you know, was always hanging around, spying on us. The priest finally told him to give us a key so we could have our programs and meetings down stairs, and we found out how to block the door so he couldn't keep sneaking in. See, in our international publication just last July, all groups were finally authorized to ordain one of our members as our priest. Well, he started snooping around and found out our *Magdalene Sister Divine* would be coming to perform the ordination of our sister and mine, Mary Anne Mahoney, who was determined to be the most pure and innocent by unanimous vote."

By now I had lost all interest in my lunch and sorely wished I still had my handbag recorder. I tried to keep my eyes from popping out of my head and kept making the required affirmative mumbling.

Mary Elizabeth was fully into her confidences, which seemed odd since I was apparently only a perspective member. It brought to mind my ex, George, who always accused me of having, that "Dear Abby" aura. She eagerly continued to share their adventure, "We had thoroughly worked with our sister Mary Anne and she had gone through all of the cleansing rituals, the purification sequence, and the sorrows and by the time *The Sister Divine* arrived, we were all prepared for the ordination. It was required that we use all of the same robes and holy chrisms or oils that are required for a priest's ordination, easy to do, since we had gained full access to everything in the church. Mary Anne would become a full priest; that must be made clear, not a priestess. Well, this Johnny person found his way into the church when we were doing our final dress rehearsal. He took photographs and just before *The Sister Divine* arrived, he tried to blackmail us, saying he would go to Father McMullen if we didn't abandon our cause.

"Strangely, the fact that we would be holding our own Masses and ordaining one of our own wasn't the main problem although he raged on about that quite violently, I might add. He was outraged that we had declared that it was Mary Magdalene who was the beloved of Jesus instead of John DeBeers' patron saint, Saint John. Well, of course we couldn't change our basic and most important fact. Blessed and Divine Mary Magdalene was of course the beloved of Jesus, as well as his wife, the mother of his children, and a co-teacher. It was sad as their ministries moved forward that she had to divorce Jesus years later when their views of salvation didn't agree. Saint Paul, a former Pharisee, of course, like today's lawyers, had the authority to handle their divorce, and then he performed the marriage later between Jesus and Lydia . . . well, John wouldn't listen to reason on any front. We don't right-out deny that there was a Saint John; just that we know he was not the Beloved and did not write what has been called *Gospel of John w*hich of course was obviously written by Mary Magdalene; nor did that John endure in the scriptures at the same elevated status as our Beloved Mary Magdalene. We have years of research that prove our facts."

Old Mary Elizabeth was on such a roll I wisely did not burst an artery by violently confronting her about her facts. Instead I kept a frozen, glass-eyed frog expression and allowed her to prattle on.

"That John person attacked Mary Martha once after a meeting, took all of our publications from her case, and burned them. He said that Saint John was his patron saint and something about how it was only Saint John and all the saints and even God himself had saved his life and the lives of hundreds of his men during all the years he spent in battle zones. As I said, we don't deny that such a person existed; just that his John was not the *Beloved of Jesus.* He had a one track mind; he allowed no room in his faith to accept anything but his own shallow view. In the end, I think he just lost his mind; you know, that Post Traumatic Stress Syndrome they talk so much about now. We've all forgiven him; Mary Martha would have wanted it that way. Poor man, he must have just gone crazy. Why that Father McMullen went along with him is what bothers us all, can you believe, a man of the cloth, our own Catholic Priest? He should have tried to do something about him but we are certain he was all behind it in the first place. He should never have been ordained in the first place and should be chastised for his lack of scriptural knowledge. Shame upon Shame!"

She finished off her plate with one big swipe with the last slice of her bread, took a final swig of her tea and stacked up the publications for me. "This has been so rewarding, my dear. Please feel free to call me or our membership chairman. All the numbers are in our leaflets. Also, go online. You'll be so filled with excitement when you read all of the wonderful things we've found on the Internet. Oh, our international web-site is listed in several places." Upon standing she patted my shoulder, "Well, dear, please feel free to finish your lunch. My tab curtains and rods are probably packaged by now and waiting for me at checkout. She then made the sign of something on my forehead. I watched her well-padded body, artfully arranged back into the good blue winter coat, waddle toward the stairs.

After my lunch, now seriously in jeopardy of not digesting, I finished my tea and shuffled through the stack of materials. This was really incredible. Could Mac have known about all of this? No wonder he'd been about to pop an artery when they kept pestering him to take over the pulpit. Did he know about the ordination, *The Sister Divine,* or had he seen any of the publications I had in front of me. I voted a very strong "no!" He would have at least turned the matter over to the Archbishop's office. I'd at least ask him that much when I would sadly report that I didn't see anyway I could possibly help his cause. Actually, they'd done nothing illegal. He'd given them full access to the church and they didn't slander any living person. In fact, they'd been quite generous in so fully forgiving poor John DeBeers. However, I was certain they were ready to hang Mac out to dry. What a mess as I kept saying, *what a freaking bloody mess!*

For a moment I thought Cal would actually be proud of me. I'd walked away unscathed. I had only given her the name of Mrs. Brown and no return telephone number and she hadn't pursued any further request for contact. She left the ball in my court. I was now certain that this group was far too strong, international, well funded, and way beyond anything I could do to change the course of their forward march. I felt sorry for poor John DeBeers sitting in jail with only the enduring hope that his patron Saint John was still out there hearing his prayers. It made me pretty sad. How easy is for someone to infringe into the deepest soul of someone's belief structure? I don't know about anyone else, but just hearing all of this from afar, so to speak, made me embrace my faith and religion and be thankful. I was far from a perfect Catholic, but I believed deeply that within the heart and mind of our Heavenly Father; he knows my heart, and for all of my sins, I believe that he loves me. I can't believe that the Bible, shared by multi-cultures and faith, would have endured without His encouragement. Anyway, I didn't see any harm in stopping by the Catholic gift shop and picking up some Saint John materials, medals, and a picture or two, nothing sharp or considered dangerous. I'd only go far enough to drop it off, unwrapped, at the jail and ask them to give it to DeBeers. He needed to know that many of us still kept our Saint John, Beloved of Christ, on our lists for intercessory prayers. Though we believed in the person of Mary Magdalene I for one had no clue what she might have done historically and I don't think anyone else, even the sacred writers of the sacred books knew either. I honestly don't believe there's enough *factual or concrete* information about her anywhere to make so many decisive and final claims regarding her life or her complete role. No one had been there taking day to day notes and planning to compile her authorized bio. If they were, I can't believe that the Magdalene's would have had the only copy.

After my lunch companion left I had some free time on my hands. Since I hadn't had yet introduced myself to Denver's latest international big box store, I moseyed around and bought some very interesting and innovative items for Mosscreek and Pam's quarters at Sam's. I smiled. She was doing so well.

I think I may have dodged a bullet when it came to Mac's trauma. I honestly, for the first time in many years, felt well, not really sad that I couldn't help someone namely Mac, but maybe also a bit relieved. Unfortunately, I patted myself on the back just a bit too soon. When I got back to my condo I had a message; Mac's attorney called me in for 'a chat regarding our priest.'

Chapter Thirteen

▼

Albert Angeletti, Esq. was a very smartly dressed, well groomed, and an efficient-looking man probably in his early sixties. He had smooth olive skin, dark eyes, prominent nose and expertly arranged dark hair with the only slightest hint of grey that made him look like . . . well like one that I could easily associate with a high-ranking member of the *Mafioso*. That of course had no bearing on the nature of the man himself; as I've said in the past, God has given me a very fertile imagination, and he had most likely been assigned to Mac by the Chancery office.

He stood and extended his hand, "Mrs. Brown; I appreciate your coming. May I offer refreshment? Wine? I think I'll have a glass, red all right? It's supposed to good for cholesterol so my wife keeps telling me".

I managed to keep nodding as he made the selection and handed me a lovely crystal goblet. He motioned to the large designer chair opposite the one he re-occupied which sat at the end of a large extremely up-market office and several oriental carpet feet from the heavy executive desk and leather side chairs. I smiled and murmured a few platitudes. I took an appreciative sip before I said, "I'll start out by admitting that I'm not really certain why I'm here. You're representing Father McMullen, I understand."

He nodded and smiled, "Yes, he has been under a great deal of stress but had been doing quite well under the circumstances, I'd believed. He spoke of you quite fondly and seems to believe that you can offer all the information necessary to have his charges dropped."

I raised my eyebrows and placed the glass on the coaster on carved mahogany table between our chairs, "Oh, goodness. I love Father Mac, we've been friends and unfortunately, co-victims in the past, but I'm certainly no miracle worker even though some situations have come to satisfactory conclusions. I'm not certain this is going to be one of them, excuse me, but you seem to be speaking of him in the past tense?

He reached for a large file folder on the table between us. "Let me bring you up to date if you'll bear with me while I fill in a few blanks." He put on a pair of round silver-rimmed 'John Lennon' type glasses and spent a moment or two flipping through a few pages. He looked up, "I understand that Father McMullen had telephoned you on two different occasions; once when he initially called you about the murder, then when he revealed that John DeBeers had passed a polygraph test in which he claimed that Father McMullen directed him to kill the Mahoney woman; and in a somewhat panic and insisted you visit him immediately, which you in fact, did."

"Yes, both of those statements are true, in fact, Father Mac told me that he had begged to take a polygraph himself but that some ruling in the church forbids a priest to be questioned when the sanctity of the confessional could be compromised. I did go to him immediately and he was in a panic, saying that he was under house arrest and was afraid of being in violation of a court order, but wanted to get away and speak to me in private."

He made a few notes, "Approximately how long were the two of you away?"

"Just long enough for a quick cup of coffee and for him to relate his fears. I'd say even less that a half hour. I really didn't want to be involved, but I felt I had to honor his request for help. There's really nothing I can do for him. I tried to explain that."

Mr. Angeletti took off his glasses and looked directly at me, "Mrs. Brown, respectfully I must ask if you care enough for Father McMullen to have been involved in his disappearance?"

I almost dropped my teeth, "Disappearance? My Lord, what has happened? Of course I had no idea that he's missing. Do we know if he's safe?" I stood up and walked over to a window overlooking Denver. I had to take a few moments to compose myself. I turned, "Whom do you suspect, certainly not me? I'm on the side of the law that I've sworn to uphold."

He made a quick gesture of assurance, "Please, I'm sorry I had to use dramatic tactics, but that's sometimes the best method. No, I don't believe you're involved; I've spoken to Mr. Cleere prior to asking you to come in and he certainly verifies your honesty and validity as well as your devotion to Father McMullen. I had ventured to ask him if he would be available to help pursue this new situation, but he assured me that you have already been involved due to your concern and friendship for our priest. He said that you would be best qualified to work with us if we deem it necessary. I would like to assume your response would be in the affirmative? He gave me a very brief overview of your meeting with the Magdalene representative, and much of what he said coincides with the report Father McMullen had sent to the Archbishop's office. He was extremely eager to remove what he believed to be a dangerous, powerful, and heretical group from his parish and concerned about their apparent international backing."

First of all, I was now in a turmoil, just having been linked to a kidnapping and then finding out that Cal was already involved, and I knew he'd been at Mosscreek working his buns off, not wasting his time keeping track of me, *and I'd promised him I'd behave!* Then I thought, hiding an internal ear-to-ear grin, *he said that about me?* My second reaction was to give him a very professional nod to acquiesce as he consulted his notes and continued with the saga.

"Father McMullen apparently disappeared two days ago from the house where he was being cared for. The brother overseeing him said he returned from a funeral on this past Monday to find the front door open, the priest gone, his snow boots and jacket on the floor by the door. Brother Sebastian said he'd been gone less than an hour. A bit longer than the time Father McMullen had previously left the house to be with you. Since that brief disappearance had gone unnoticed by Brother Sebastian, he would have had no reason to suspect there might be a breach, so to say, in the secure environment we've attempted to create for the priest. We've tried to shield him from newsmongers and have been taking precautions just in the event of any sort of danger. One never knows what might happen when a priest's name hits the media."

Horrific but true, I mused. God save us all from fabricated stories and accusations, and the horror of abhorrent truths.

He closed his folder, "At this point, there has been no word regarding his whereabouts. We have no additional leads. I might add that the church women in that Mary cult have been thoroughly questioned; perhaps though not all of them as you know they are a rather closed society. Additionally, we understand he was expecting his sister to arrive from Florida at some point. We've checked all arrivals and departures everywhere from airlines, trains, and busses. No arrivals or departures of anyone fitting Father McMullen's' description, no single elderly women has arrived from Florida around that time period; of course in a city as large as ours, it would be impossible to discern that as a fact. She could have arrived from anywhere. As you can see, we have a problem on our hands. We did not consider him a flight risk, but instead had him in protective custody considering that Magdalene group had insisted that he had a hand in the murder of their leader."

For the next half hour I went over with him my meeting with the Magdalene representative that I'd met at IKEA. I gave him all of the publications she'd left with me and at the end of our meeting. He briefly perused them and by the time we'd neared the end of our meeting, he seemed far more concerned for Father Mac's safety than he had in the beginning.

He put his folder aside, "I met with John DeBeers' attorney last week. You may have heard of him, Paul Snyder?"

I shook my head, "I don't think I know of him, off hand. Is he good?"

Angeletti nodded, "He's an outstanding criminal defense man, a highly decorated veteran and a strong and outspoken advocate for the rights of disabled veterans. He most always steps up for cases similar to this one. He is taking on DeBeers and from working with him in the past, I've found that he will leave no stone unturned until he's satisfied that his clients have the very best representation he can provide. He works Pro Bono on these cases and doesn't care how long they take. I think he'll uncover information that could be helpful to us. By the way, he said that DeBeers' two daughters had contacted him to say they will be arriving in Denver and stay throughout the procedures regarding their father's arrest."

I sighed, "From what I understand from Mac, it is bloody well time for those two to rear their heads. The impression that Johnny gave Mac was that when he returned home the wife and daughters no longer wanted to be involved with him. For his sake I hope he got it wrong, otherwise, he's probably completely on his own. I sighed, "Mr. Angeletti, with all due respect, you've asked me here to go over all of this information, but what in the world can I do? I certainly don't have the resources available that you do, I'm not an officer of the law and I'm not an expert in missing persons."

He stood and I did as well, "Ms. Brown, you've already met with the upcoming leader of the Magdalenes, perhaps you could continue visiting with members of the group and glean further information, casually of course, of their plans, in a professional capacity of course.

"Mr. Cleere and I established an amount for your retainer." He handed me an envelope, "I don't believe them to be dangerous or I wouldn't suggest having you involved. As I said, the police have questioned the members they were able to locate, but they are not forthcoming with information about other members. They have no membership log, so they say, and we cannot harass them to weed out other women who may be involved or have helpful information. Perhaps you could continue with your tentative relationship and present yourself as interested in their work, possibly even obtaining an invitation to a meeting? Mr. Cleere says you can be quite thorough and persuasive, and I know he meant that as a validation of your abilities. I'm somewhat certain that if they are holding our priest somewhere; they wouldn't be resorting to torture or murder, perhaps more suggestive of a penitential sort of imprisonment. We don't actually believe that they are holding him nor that are they violent; a bit strange and gullible perhaps, but surely no more than that. If for a moment you find yourself uncomfortable with the assignment, then by all means, please step aside at once and call me. The police think Father McMullen and his sister have likely done a runner and left clues behind to make it look like he left unwillingly. We know the fellow has enough on his plate to want to run away and his sister seems to be the sort to have already had it planned. In any case we'll do what we can as we wait for new information. I appreciate your willingness to offer your assistance, here's my card with my private cell." He handed the publications from the Magdalenes back to me with a smile.

As I rode back down to the glassed and marbled lobby, I realized that he didn't actually give enough pause in his long discourse to allow me to refuse, and I did take the publications and the retainer he handed back to me. That in itself was a form of agreement; but then, he already knew that I was chomping at the bit to help Mac.

✶   ✶   ✶   ✶

I sat in my SUV and decided to relax a while and enjoy the prime parking space I'd snagged just off the 16th Street Mall. I pulled the top flyer out of my bag and studied the information published by the local chapter of the Magdalenes. I folded it over so the email address was clearly visible. If I was going to keep my cover, I'd have to do a couple of things; first of all, get a PO Box. My address must absolutely remain private. Secondly, my driver's license stated my legal name as Madge Middleton Brown. I'd have to open the box in at least the first two names and fill out their informational application likewise. I sat for a few minutes enjoying the hustle and bustle of the noonday activities in and out of the restaurants and boutiques while I pondered my fate. Cal's warnings reverberated in my head as I pulled away from the curb and headed to the branch post office near Cal's office. It was always busy and a good place to use for a cover. Half an hour later with the box secured and payment receipt in hand I decided to go back to my condo and continue packing the dishes and linens I wanted to transfer to Mosscreek.

With a couple of stacks of boxes that were ready to transfer to the back of my vehicle, I was sorting through my bookshelf when Cal called, "Middy, can you get away for a few days? There are quite a few things here at Mosscreek that need your input. I thought you might bring down a few of the boxes I left in the bedroom of my condo; I'm running out of clothes."

There I was again, between a rock and a hard place, I frowned, "Uh, excuse me, didn't we install washers and dryers last year, I know they almost work by themselves, you've been a bachelor for how long . . . ?"

He laughed, "Okay, but I actually tore out last time to meet with the contractor with only the clothes on my back . . . does that satisfy you, besides, some things shouldn't wait, can you drive down?"

We chatted a minute and then I added, "The only problem I see is that I just left Angeletti's office and he wants me to meet with those Magdalenes. I think you already know about that, though; and the news is that Father Mac is missing. He's been gone for several days."

"Damn! He was all right when I talked to Angeletti earlier in the week. What's happened?"

I filled him in the details I'd been told and ended with, "Bottom line, no one knows and all inquiries turn up nothing. I'm supposed to infiltrate the Magdalenes and pretend to be interested in joining them and see if I can ferret out any information or gain any clue that they might be holding Mac. I can't come just now."

He swore, "I did absolutely not want it to come to this, but I did tell Angeletti that you had already made inroads into that group. I'm sorry if I set you up. How soon can you get away?"

Thinking fast I came up with an alternative plan, "The application for membership is online. Why don't I just fill it out and email it to the local group. It should take them a few days to process it. I've done everything under Madge Middleton and rented a PO Box so I'll be able to be as anonymous as possible. I'll set up another email account. In fact, I'll do that and come to Mosscreek late this afternoon and stay until I hear something from them online."

CHAPTER FOURTEEN

▼

A quick stop at the supermarket filled eight stretchy bags with quick-fix provisions, a few bottles of okay wine, coffee makings, and assorted snacks and beverages. It was almost dark when I pulled into the circular drive. All the contractor vehicles were gone and I took a moment to savor the surroundings and take a deep breath of the gentle fragrance of burning logs drifting above the tall, brick chimney. Cal came out immediately and we lugged in the groceries and in less than a half hour, we were having microwave dinners, enjoying wine, and warming toes in front of the fire.

The east side of the house was a mess but it looked fantastic. The new staircase was almost finished and Cal wouldn't let me venture up. The room we were in that was to be our private study downstairs was now situated behind a beautiful antique door. With all my concerns behind me, I looked forward even more than I'd imagined to these few days borrowed from my future.

After a few hours enjoying the quiet and catching up on all that had happened since we'd last seen one another, Cal became rather reflective, "Sweetheart, this is horrific and I'm sorry. I wanted to save this until tomorrow but I don't think that's being fair . . . we've had to stop working on the upstairs reconfiguration, that's why I was so insistent about you coming down."

"Why? Cal, what's happened, what's wrong?"

He took my hand, "The police and coroner will be coming out first thing in the morning. Remember I said we should be able to enlarge one of the areas because the external measurements didn't come out right?"

I nodded, "Vaguely, keep going, coroner? what's happened?"

"We found the human skeletal remains of two adults and what could possibly be two children in the far recesses at the near end of that wall. The contractors took off immediately when they pulled down the paneling, and by the time I got them calmed down, sorted out and they left, I called the police and then called you. The remains appear to have been in that location for many, many years. Obviously, it's a crime scene. The police ordered us to stop all work and seal the room until they arrive. I identified myself and assured them they didn't need to come out until tomorrow and I'd verify that nothing had been or would be touched. Since it is apparent that the bodies were hidden and then closed in, we should stay away, the murderer may have dusted the closet with traces of lime. I know you won't want to go upstairs tonight, so I fixed up the downstairs maid's room. That's why I wouldn't let you climb up the new stairs. I knew you'd have a problem with what we've found. This is an old, old crime scene, Middy; we've been here over a year without knowing about it, so please, let's just keep our imaginations out of it. We may never get to the bottom of it."

"But Cal, what about poor Clarissa Bonforte, this was her home, did it happen while she lived here? Was she involved? This is too horrible . . . !"

He took my hand and led me into the kitchen and mixed up a nice Hot Toddy. I sat at the kitchen table trying to hold it in my trembling hands. I needed some things out of the car but I couldn't make myself go even as far as the entryway. I was immediately a seven year old, afraid of the dark and absolutely positive that I'd see ghosts coming down the stairs if I went back into the hallway again. Cal had carried down some of the personal items I'd put in the drawers of the old dresser upstairs and had laid them out on the bench in the maid's room. I didn't even want to touch them, childishly believing that they'd been handled by murdered ghosts. I slugged down my drink letting it practically scorch my throat, went into the downstairs bathroom for quick bedtime prep and tried to keep from gagging. After I splashed water on my face I ran for the bed and burrowed under the heavy quilt, "Leave the light on . . . no, turn it off, no . . ."

Cal had followed me and sighed and shook his head, but laughed lightly, "Middy, we've been sleeping here for a while now and they haven't come out or bothered anyone yet, surely you don't believe in that nonsense."

With my head further under the covers my muffled voice called out, "Yeah, but now you've taken out the wall!" I started crying, "My beautiful Mosscreek, it's ruined, I felt so safe here, it's just not fair, it's not fair!"

I gave into my grief; I couldn't make myself behave and I knew I was being childish and was well aware that I had consumed libations enough to simply let myself go. I guess sometimes that just needs to happen, the childishness, not the libations. I sobbed into the quilt ignoring Cal's attempts to reassure me . . . Fortunately, after a while, he was able to calm me down and put me to sleep.

*   *   *   *

Car doors slamming and strange voices woke me from my deep, troubled sleep. My surroundings were different and momentarily I was disoriented; and then with a vengeance I remember what had happened and why I was in the room off the kitchen. There was a slight tap on the door and Gracie Haggis peeked through the opening, "You awake now, dearie?"

She walked over to the bed as I was struggled to sit upright. "Oh, Gracie, have they told you?"

Gracie began fussing with the bedding, smoothing it over my feet and fluffing the pillows behind me, "Shush now, dearie. Calvin has the police upstairs and they've brought along the corner's photographer and her van. Don't worry now, they have everything under control. He told Benny that it would all be cleared out by noon and then the two of them could finish taking down that awful wall. He asked me to be sure that you stay right here in this room. He doesn't want you seeing anything that's going to leave you with bad memories."

He was right. I actually didn't even want to get out of bed, but Gracie was already in the adjoining bathroom filling the tub. Within a few seconds the gentle scent of lavender wafted into the bedroom.

She came out drying her hands on her apron, "I'll have a nice breakfast for you right here on your little table when you get out of the tub. I'll listen for you. You just relax. I'll tell Calvin that you're awake and that you promised to stay in your room until he comes for you, until then, you should try to take a little nap after breakfast, watch a bit of the tellie, or read your little electric book. I'll be checking on you if you want anything. I'll bring in the electric coffee pot and extra muffins so there's no need for you to fuss. Just relax." With that, she left the room and gently closed the door behind her.

By noon I was pacing the floor. I heard car doors again, voices, the front door opening and closing, and had to fight to keep my imagination from running away with me. I opened the door a fraction and called for Gracie. She came in, again wiping her hands on her apron and the delicious aroma of cooking drifted in. I asked her if she would sit down and visit with me. I'd been growing antsier by the minute. She hurried back into the kitchen to tend to her cooking and then took off her apron and carried in an extra cup. She poured her coffee from the generous hot pot and we both sat down on the heavily upholstered and high-backed Queen Anne chairs.

I needed distraction, "Gracie, talk to me about anything, in fact, tell me about Clarissa, how you met her . . . I need to feel her in the house, now more than ever, and I saw her so very briefly before she died. Poor thing, to think of all she didn't know about. At least that was a blessing, I guess."

She smiled, "Dear Miss Bonforte, Oh, my goodness, you're practically asking me to go back to my childhood, well let me see where to start:

She was clearly pleased to share her story and put her cup down on the table and folded her hands in her lap, "You see, I was the youngest of five daughters and we all grew up on the farm, just up in Northern Colorado. We learned to work like boys, but by and by the older girls got married and some stayed on the farm, their husbands taking over the chores. Harvest time was a busy time and they always hired extra help. Well, that's how I met Benny. He had lived with his old grandpa who had just died, he'd been a tough old Scotsman and Benny said he drank himself to death. Anyway he'd been a good provider and a very dear man. Now that Benny was eighteen, he decided to sell off their little house and join the Army. But on account of an old broken ankle that didn't heal right, they wouldn't take him." She smiled in fond recollection and I was beginning to relax and tried to ignore the distant sounds coming from the other end of the house.

"As it turned out, by the time the harvesting was over, Benny and I had fallen in love. I was just barley sixteen. Not being mean or anything, I believe my folks was quite relieved when we asked permission to marry since they already had so many mouths to feed, ya' know. By then Benny had put aside the money from selling his grandpa's house and he had the old truck they'd used to deliver eggs, that's what they did, raise chickens and sell eggs; so with his farm wages and money in the bank, we thought we was millionaires." She paused to laugh, "Lands, we was green as grass!

"Anyways, we was sitting in the Court House waiting our turn to get married and was talking a bit between the two of us about what we was going to do since we didn't have no idea now that we had come that far. And wouldn't you know it, sitting right there waiting her turn to take care of some business about buying Mosscreek sat the perkiest and most beautiful young woman I'd ever laid eyes on. Oh, and she was bold, made no bones about listening to us talking amongst ourselves. Finally she comes over and says, 'I need a handyman and a woman to take care of my new house. There's a cottage and good pay if you want the jobs.' Well, goodness, we like to have fell right over on the spot. Long story made short, we jumped at the chance, and a couple of hours later we was sitting in her big old black Rolls Royce at the Big Boy Hamburger place laughing and eating our wedding lunch."

I had closed my eyes, occasionally making a comment while trying to visualize her story. Oh, how I regretted being deprived of the opportunity to know Clarissa for more than three brief encounters. Gracie refilled our cups and reenergized she continued, "This is the thing, here we was, a couple of kids sitting in this big car laughing with this beautiful girl, well, she was hardly even twenty-four years old and she and Benny was smoking big, fat cigars just as smart as you please. She was wearing as fine a dress as I ever saw and a smart little cloche hat. She acted like she was the most carefree person in the whole wide world. I said how much I liked her hat and she snubbed out her cigar and started up the car, 'Well then, you shall have one just like it if you wish.' Course, I was embarrassed, I didn't mean anything to come back to me, and I was just so taken up with her. Next thing I know, we're at that great big Sears and Roebuck or maybe it was a Montgomery Ward store that used to be downtown, maybe somewhere on Broadway, I don't remember anymore. Anyway, she bought me and Benny work clothes, jackets, shoes, boots, dress up outfits—she said Benny could be her butler when she had company; course we had no idea what she was referring to; and we each got grand hats, one special for Benny since she said he was to start driving her around, and for me, a pretty red coat and a hat like the one she wore, or least ways nearly like it. Well, we was flabbergasted. Course later on, we learned that she had just got back to Denver from some real fancy boarding school back East and her Ma and Pa had money to burn. They sure gave a fair share to her, their only child. Lands, I couldn't imagine having no sisters and all that money instead. Her Pa had something to do with the railroads and breeding some special beef cattle at his ranch down in Texas. As long as she lived, she always had more money to spend than the bank."

"Gracie, was she writing her poetry at that age?"

She laughed, "Oh lands yes. Why, there was one of them speckled black and white lesson books laid everywhere all over the house. Sometimes she'd come running in the house with the dogs on her heels, kick off her shoes and grab one of them books and get started on writing and nothing else would enter her mind. She'd forget to close the door, feed the dogs, shutter the windows, and even eat once she had an idea for a poem. Oftentimes I wonder if I still don't hear the click of her heels as she walked from one end of the house to the other reading her new poem out loud to make sure the rhythm, she called it, was just right. When she got so old and decided to move to that care home, she boxed up all them lesson books and give them to me. I have them in our little attic. I can't bring myself to bring them down. Maybe someday you and me can look through them. Course, that was before the trouble. After that nothing ever got back to exactly the same as them happy days. But, she took things in stride, somehow. She was wonderful clear up to the end. There won't never be another like her"

Startled I sat upright and turned to her, "Trouble? Like that business upstairs?"

"Oh no, gracious no, now you don't be troubling yourself about that upstairs business. Mosscreek is full of happy memories. You can even feel it in the air. It ain't the fault of a house if troubles come in the door. The folks what live in it have to listed real carful in the quiet of the morning, or in the late afternoon when the breeze has settled down, or even at night while sitting in front of the fire. You know they say that sounds never die. Miss Bonforte's lovely voice reading her poems out loud, the click of her heels, all the happy times when her friends was here, playing the piano, dancing, reading their own poems, laughing, chiding one another; them are the things the house hears, them are the things that lasts forever. The troubles come and leave a mark, but they're soon gone; it's the heart of the house and the memories it keeps that it wants you to live with."

"But the troubles?" I persisted, "what happened?"

She stood and gathered up the coffee cups, "Now, don't you be fretting. We'll talk another time. I think some of them cars have come and gone. I'll check with Calvin. I'm leaving a nice crock-pot of beef stew for your supper and I brought over a loaf of fresh bread and an apple pie I baked this morning early. It looks like there's a few things you brought with you in the icebox so I didn't make up anything for your lunch." With that she gave me a sweet smile and left the room.

The boxes and suitcase I'd brought down from the condos were stacked against the wall. I rummaged through and pulled out a pair of jeans and a sweatshirt. My feet were just fine in the hiking socks I'd pulled on after my bath so I did a quick hair and face fix and took out my *Kindle*. I would stand by my promise and stay comfortably confined. But this thought brought to mind Father Mac. I slipped out my laptop and logged in.

There were no new emails so I pursued the news. It was heartbreaking to acknowledge how much crime had moved into Denver over the years; like all big cities, probably. I'd worried all of my life that something horrible would happen to the kids. I offered a quick prayer that we had managed to weather all the storms thus far; and there had been storms. I logged out. Father Mac had already had his fifteen minutes of fame, either that, or Angeletti had pulled some strings to keep his disappearance quiet. I doubted that our unwelcome guests in the closet upstairs would merit any coverage either, at least until we had some answers. I wanted to protect our privacy and Mosscreek. I hoped Cal had been able to make that clear. I didn't want media coverage. I wanted to reclaim Mosscreek as my own.

In light of my present imprisonment, I really wanted to go back to the condo. I had no desire to think about any further remodel projects for a while. Cal could take over completely. I didn't ever want to identify my upstairs space with whatever area had been involved. If he'd told me, I had thankfully forgotten. Father Mac was on my mind now, I wanted to get the Magdalene interviews over quickly and turn the Mac thing over to the powers that be; actually I wanted to leave Denver proper soon and try to find peace here at Mosscreek, this was just not the time, I wasn't nearly as strong as I'd always believed I was. Cal would have to understand. I rummaged through the things

I'd brought down and repacked the suitcase. By the time Cal came back, I'd made my decision to leave right away. I didn't want to spend another night in the house until he had removed everything connected to this new incident. When he finally came into the room, I didn't give him the opportunity to fill me in on anything.

"Cal, I have to go back home. Please understand, you take care of everything here, the decisions, and the construction, all of it. I don't want to know anything else. Call me when this is behind us. I know I'm being childish. I want to see Pam and Sam; I want to try to get back to normal. I want to cleanse my mind. I want to be a happy bride. That's not going to happen with all this going on upstairs."

He shook his head, "Middy, please . . ."

I put my fingers to his lips and then kissed him. "Understand, please. I need to shake this off and I can't reason with myself here."

CHAPTER FIFTEEN

▼

The sun was shining and slowly the snow began melting. The typical late winter muddy slush would hang around all day and by early evening, just when the after work crowd hit the roads, the temperature would have dropped dramatically and black ice would become the dangerous norm on the sidewalks and roadways. Pam and I were enjoying a hot latté with a natural grain, cream cheese and sprouts sandwich. We'd just selected the dresses for next week's wedding and were ultra conscious of our calorie intake in light of the fact that our dresses were now in the alterations department. I had our marriage license and I'd just picked up Cal's wedding ring from the jeweler. I was feeling that deep down happiness that those soon to be married can claim as their very own; or so I had imagined. I gently touched my purse where I had tucked them both away . . . like a silly schoolgirl, probably.

My trip last week back to Mosscreek hadn't brought me actual closure. That might never happen. However, I did go upstairs and wander through the new bedroom suite and office configuration, and since I didn't actually know where the offensive find had been located, and Cal chose not to reveal it, I was very happy with the new layout. He and the contractor had completely torn down some of the framed walls I had last seen and the new areas with the drywall and texturing in place looked wonderful. We made a final selection of the paint colors and I'd brought along the wallpaper I'd ordered for my dressing area and Cal said he'd hang it. I called him my man of many undisclosed talents and he had a very smart-alecky, personal comeback. Men!

I ventured to ask Cal about what the police had located about the upstairs finding, and he said they would be going back over missing persons reports from the 1940's, or earlier; but that at this time it was a very low priority. A lot more testing had to be done before anything could be finalized. I decided to let it drop.

Pam was happy again. She sipped her latté and nibbled on her sandwich in between giving me updates on how she was settling into her new world. It seemed a bit odd that my daughter would be excited about the details of her mother's wedding instead of the other way around, but hearing her enthusiasm so soon after her trauma just made me realize what a fantastic young woman she had become.

My cell phone wiggled around in my pocket, I didn't want it to ring in the middle of our luncheon, but seeing that the caller was Mr. Angeletti, I gestured to Pam and answered. After several breath intakes and biting my tongue to keep from interrupting, he told me that Father Mac had been found wandering the street not far from Brother Sebastian's house, without a coat and carrying what he called a blindfold. He appeared to be well but had no idea where he had been nor had any concept of how long he'd been gone. And, could I possibly visit him at the brother's house on my first opportunity since he'd been asking for me, in fact, could we meet there at eight o'clock in the morning since he and the police were there with him today? Whew! He added that in addition, now that Father Mac was available, the judge had cleared a time on Friday when the prosecution and defense could state their cases and decisions could be made. He thought it would be fine if I wished to attend and he would let me know before hand if all could be arranged that quickly.

Poor Mac! Brother Sebastian opened the door and introduced himself. He said that Father Mac had been up since six o'clock waiting for me to arrive. He offered breakfast which I declined and he led me to the sitting room where Mac was watching a morning news show, "Madge, oh Praise God, I've been found!" He pulled himself up from a comfortable easy chair and threw his arms around me. "I never prayed so hard in my life. Here, sit down, we need you to find out where I've been."

I laughed, "Father Mac, except for your longish hippy hair, you look fantastic . . . rested, well nourished, and I venture to say, happy,"

"Oh, you just don't know, wait till I tell you everything . . ."

I interrupted, "Mr. Angeletti said he would join me here, shouldn't we wait for him?" At that moment the door bell rang and Mac reached for the remote and turned off the TV set. Mr. Angeletti came in shod of coat and we shook hands all around.

For want of something to do during the pleasantries, I took out a small notepad and pencil and waited to be addressed.

"Madge, I thought of so much more this morning than I did yesterday. I was kidnapped, you know, can you believe it?"

Angeletti visited with us for a minute and asked Mac to start again at the beginning and let us know what else he may have remembered. He started on his story:

"I don't remember what time of day it was, but we hadn't received **The Denver Post** yet. It was terribly late. Brother Sebastian had called it in and slipped over to the seminary to pick up something or other. In the meantime, I had ventured out onto the porch and had gone down the steps to see if it had ended up in those pesky juniper bushes. I'd just bent over when something went over my head and two people grabbed me and carried me to a vehicle that was idling. I had my glasses on the cord around my neck and it was starting to choke me. I tried to yell. They put me in the back seat and one of them got in beside me and while she—it was a woman—(Angeletti and I exchanged looks) buckled me in, the vehicle zoomed away into traffic. I kept asking who they were and what they wanted, but no one would answer me. Finally I just started praying to myself and tried to feel for my rosary. I couldn't get it all the way out of my pocket for the seatbelt and the woman beside me wiggled it loose and gave it to me. Well, I figured either they were going to let me be in peace, or I'd be resting in peace." He chuckled at his little joke. He was obviously in very good spirits, in a comfortable environment, and anxious to share his adventure.

"We drove for a really long time. The woman had pushed me down in the seat and I knew I'd best behave. At last we drove over a bump and I heard the sound of a garage door. The vehicle stopped and I was unbuckled. Still without a word, I was pulled by the arm to indicate that I was supposed to get out. Oh, before the woman pushed me down on the seat, she slipped off whatever had been over my head and quickly tied a blindfold tightly around my eyes. In that brief second, I saw the upholstery in front of my face was tan leather." He smiled, "I learned some tricks from you, Madge Brown!" I jotted that down on my notepad.

"Then, a door opened and they led me into the house, finally someone said, 'step up, again, again.' Then I was led through a room with hard floor, it sounded like old linoleum, and then another door opened and the person leading me said, 'downstairs.' I could feel it was much colder and figured they were going to lock me in a basement. When we got to the bottom, someone switched on a light and said I would find everything I needed to be comfortable and to make myself at home. The only instruction was that when they called for me to put the blindfold back on, I was to do that or they wouldn't bring down any food. And of course the obvious, the door would be locked so unless I wanted trouble, I'd best cooperate. So, for the rest of my time there, I did that. I knew it wouldn't do any good to yell for help because they might decide to dope me up or maybe knock me out, so I decided to cooperate fully."

Angeletti spoke, "Since yesterday, have you remembered anything about the two people? Did you overhear any names, or have the chance to see anyone?"

Mac made a thoughtful face, "You know, I remember cowboy boots, roughed up ones, brown. I could see down under the blindfold sometimes, and I did see that. Also sometimes when the brown boot one, who was the only one who ever came down, it was always the same voice; and once the door wasn't quite shut, I could hear the one upstairs talking on the phone. Oh yeah, it was another woman; I know I plainly heard what she had been saying, but right now I just can't remember what it was, I seem to remember that 'furniture' was mentioned. I'm sorry."

Angeletti remained silent, I spoke up, "Mac, what about the room where you were held?"

"Oh, it was nice I suppose. It was a whole basement. It had a bedroom and a bathroom, quite comfortable. A little table and chair with shelves along the wall with a lot of boxed puzzles and odds and ends of things. I worked quite a few of them, the puzzles. And there were old books, some of the Classics. I enjoyed them; since Seminary I've never got a chance to read too many. The other end was closed off with a door, but it wasn't locked. It was just storage. I snooped around a bit but it was just old memory stuff and Christmas decorations, that kind of thing, never saw anything with a name or any identification. There were a couple of green army-like lockers and a trunk or two buried under some heavy boxes, too heavy for me to life down, but they were probably all locked and I didn't want to get caught snooping. After the first couple of days they brought me down some jeans and heavy shirts and some socks, even a pair of pretty good slippers and a nice sweater. I figured they'd gone to the thrift store as it was all used."

"And, what was your overall impression of your stay?" This had been Angeletti.

Mac shook his head, "Darned if I can figure it out; at first I was pretty scared. I crawled on some boxes in that storage room so I could reach a window. They were those really old small ones like in old houses, anyway, the windows were completely dusted over and sealed shut. I wrote 'HELP ME' on one, only to remember that from the outside it would be backwards, so I climbed up to reach the other one and figured out how to write it so it would read right. Course, I hoped the women didn't find it and I almost started to rub it off, but decided to take a chance. Other than that and being confined like a monk, I really couldn't complain. I missed Carmen's cooking of course, but I found that a lot of those Hungry Fellow microwave dinners were pretty darn good. They brought me a lot of pizza and even brought me one with anchovies one time when I asked. I got to read, nap, no phone, no television, nobody with problems. All in all, I didn't really mind it. I'd pretty much decided they weren't going to hurt me. They'd thought of everything I might need, toothbrush, shaver, deodorant, like those little things you get when you're in the hospital. There was even laundry soap in the bathroom and I washed my clothes out in the bathtub or sink and rigged up a pole from the storage to prop up and use for a clothes dryer. I got to soak in the tub without interruptions, and nowadays, you have to admit that almost nobody can do that anymore. Course I prayed constantly that poor Johnny would tell the police the truth and I would be released. I thought it was funny that I got kidnapped from one safe house and was then kept in another. After a while, I wondered if the two were related. I just don't know."

Angeletti, "And the day you were released, what about that?"

"It was strange. They brought me down a really good breakfast; home cooked this time, and my pot of coffee. I'd been told to put my empty tray always on the top step of the stairs, and that day I did the same thing but I never heard anyone pick it up. I thought for a while they'd gone off and I was alone. About the time I thought I'd try the door, I heard the 'blindfold' order and the sound of Brown Boots coming down the stairs. She said, 'upstairs now' and I started getting really scared. It ran through my mind that they had been holding me for ransom, but then I figured nobody, even the Vatican, would part with a thin dime to pay for my release. It made me sad and I pretty well just gave in to my fate; I'm an old man and can't be of any use to anyone anymore.

"Anyway, we got back in the vehicle and I was buckled in. After a time, the vehicle stopped and I was unbuckled and told to get out. I was shaking like a leaf and was starting to get nauseous. I was afraid this was the hostage trade off or I was going to be killed. Then I was led to what felt like a sidewalk, I still had on the slippers, and Brown Boots started turning me around till I was getting dizzy. She told me to sit down. I heard her walk away and then the vehicle sped off. I heard traffic like I was near a street so I peeked out from my blindfold and saw that I was alone, sitting down on the sidewalk next to the curb. I was still dizzy so I waited till I could stand up. I walked to the corner and tried to ask a person waiting to cross the street to call the police for me. They shrugged me off and crossed the street. I wandered around the neighborhood and had no idea where I was. I asked people at the bus stop where we were but I guess they thought I was some homeless person and they just shook their heads at me and turned away. That's all I really remember except that I was freezing cold."

Angeletti finished the tale, "Someone called the police from a non-traceable number and said you could be found somewhere around the neighborhood. The police came and scoured the area until you were found. After a lot of back and forth decisions, they took you to Brother Sebastian's. Then they called me.

Father Mac just shook his head. "What was the point behind this? I just can't imagine, what was the point?" I'd made copious notes, not knowing what good they were going to be, but I thought something might be helpful.

After a long silence, Angeletti spoke, "Yesterday I was called to meet with DeBeer's attorney, Paul Snyder, and the Prosecution team to discuss our case. The judge has granted an early hearing tomorrow at seven thirty in the morning since he has a full calendar for the day. Snyder has brought in a number of consultants to visit with DeBeers, including an expert in the Post Traumatic Stress Syndrome from the Walter Reed Army Hospital Traumatic Stress Clinic. At this point we're just in the discussion stage plotting our strategy. Snyder's physician friend said it appears to be the delayed result of trauma; whether it's his tours of duty, his injuries, or both, or his encounter with the Mahoney woman, his family, or all of the above. He's most likely tragically scarred inside and out. None of our troops deserve this but war is war. It's not politically correct to question whether they are actually making a difference in light of eternity. Anyway, our man is very well controlled and respectful. He answers Snyder's questions but we aren't in that loop yet."

Mac put his head down in his hands and mumbled, "Poor Johnny, poor, poor Johnny."

Angeletti, added, "The way this is progressing and without additional proof other than DeBeers' statement, Father McMullen, I'm quite certain I can get the charges against you, whatever they are going to be, dropped."

Then quite understandably, Mac burst into tears.

Chapter Sixteen

▼

February 14th dawned bright and clear. My wake-up call had been a mushy one from Cal, deliberately silly but wonderful. Red roses had arrived at nine sharp with a beautiful card. Pam had wanted to drive to the ceremony with me so she'd come back to the condo after our morning appointments at our beauty stops and then after the ceremony would go home from the hotel with Geo or the grandparents. We had all of our beautiful dresses and accessories in my condo so we could dress and primp together.

The transportation and attendance plans were as simple as we could manage. Cal and Geo were to have stayed at Sam's last night for male bonding of some sort. Son-in-law Dan was to serve as best man and all would be in gray suits, I vetoed tuxes. I wanted the children to be present; hopefully this would be the only marriage they would witness for their grandfather.

Matt and Bruce were in charge of Mother and Dad who would take a break from their *Rio Grande Valley Polka Championship Dance-Off* and fly up, but for only one night . . . schedules had to be maintained (!) When I'd congratulated Daddy about their fifth ranking in the Dance-Off, he made me laugh, "Hell, we're bound to make it to the Grande Finale. We're the only group that can make it through a full set with our knee and hip replacements working and the oxygen tanks close enough that we can take a whiff during the applause breaks; plus we have the smarts to put our meds into liquid form so that in the event of a medical emergency you can grab a quick swig. All that's nothing compared to the poor fellow who has to do-sa-do around his colostomy bag. You know your mother and all the old gals down here, if you can halfway breathe on your own and stand upright for at least five minutes, then by damn you're gonna dance!"

*　　　*　　　*　　　*

All in all, the wedding was to be a simple affair. We had a lounge area reserved at the hotel so we could all relax and have cocktails, and later enjoy a leisurely and extravagant dinner and of course, a small wedding cake, courtesy of the *Brown Palace.*

I drove out to Sam and Dan's lovely home and picked up Pam. She said Cal had taken all the guys to Mosscreek for the morning.

Pam and I had scheduled a busy day; manicure and pedicure at ten, hair at *Salon Jorj* at noon, Court House at three. When I arrived Sam insisted that I take time for a croissant and coffee. Little Jason climbed up on my lap and was full of little-guy talk. I finally had to ask what he was trying to tell me. Sam said she and Pam had been trying to help him say 'Nana Middy' but what he had managed was *Mina,* and that was what he was telling me, that I was *Mina.* I don't know that I've ever heard anything so precious, spoken around a mouth full of bread and jelly, nor a hug and kiss sweeter than the one he delivered with an extra smudge of strawberry.

About a year ago, just when everything seemed to be coming down on me, I asked *Jorj* for a short, easy to maintain hairstyle. He'd hemmed and hawed, in Spanish of course, because he considered his original work had been perfect, but he gave me a soft shorter style that I could just gel up when in a hurry. When we arrived for our appointments, Jorj tossed my overgrown tresses here and there with consternation. I told him that I now also had the dilemma of finding more of those unwarranted pesky gray hairs sprouting out here and there and that I knew I was far overdue for a color touch-up. After his brushing and hair flipping and tossing; he agreed that a new look, especially for my wedding day, was in order. He drilled me about my dress, its style, of course, the designer, and the jewelry I would be wearing. After he had processed that information into the proper cells in his stylized brain, he shaped up my overgrown mop, had his assistants foil color my hair, but only enough to keep from completely blending in the gray around my face. They used some sort of treatment to brighten the gray and make it shine which, when I saw the final result, was actually rather wonderful. I hadn't wanted to do something completely different for the wedding, but it looked so nice that I was certain I'd made the right decision.

Jorj actually cut Pam's hair himself, and while I was under the coloring foils, Pam had a few sun streaks put in hers. We both looked pretty fantastic. After a quick stop for lunch, we headed back home to dress.

I loved my dress! It had a fitted top with a low, scooped neck which with my reconstruction surgery, came just low enough to make my upper body look quiet beautiful. There were very soft tucks of sheer voile on the bodice and the sleeves were almost transparent and long, ending with a little bracelet tuck just below the wrist bone. The skirt had multiple layers of voile overlapping one another all of different lengths and falling randomly from the softly belted waist, leaving the lower rounded hems of the skirt somewhat open and creating an extremely elegant lower leg exposure; the longest layers dropped to just above the ankle, the soft shorter ones, just below the knee. Oh, and it was an icy silvery gray that enhanced the delicate, gossamer movements when I walked.

Pam's dress was by the same designer. She chose a more simple line in a dusty pale blue-gray. She wanted something she could wear to college functions.

Instead of bouquets we chose wrist corsages, especially with the delicate fabric of our dresses, and left the choice of actual florals to Cal. He wanted to pick up the flowers and had ordered corsages for all the other female attendants and the boutonnières for the men.

When Pam and I were ready to leave, we looked so very elegant that I almost for a moment wished that we'd chosen a more personal or elaborate venue than the judge's chambers. As it turned out, our Judge Judith Westwood turned out to be quiet a romantic and assured us she was very much looking forward to meeting all the family. Obviously, she adored Cal. He had worked with her on what he indicated had been a personal matter. He said we were the last ones on her calendar for the day and she had encouraged him to bring in any 'props' that he wanted. He had the rental company deliver a bridal arch decorated with sheer fabric and two tall baskets of lovely silk flowers. He paid for them to wait until the ceremony finished and then take them away again. The photographer we had engaged managed to get several fantastic photos with the rented background set which was an unexpected treat. All in all, it was quite wonderful.

Judge Judy had me enter on Geo's arm and we have a great photo of him placing my hand in Cal's. All three and a half of our men stood side by side, little Jason in his first suit held the box with the ring which he handed to his daddy like a little pro. Pam was so beautiful. Mother and Dad of course, had no idea of what she had just been through and it was wonderful to see them so enchanted with their beautiful granddaughter. Matt's kids were both away at school, so Geo and Pam spend extra time fussing over their grandparents. We have wonderful photographs of our family at the wedding in formal pose, and also at the hotel with their magnificent décor, the perfect backdrop to create memories. Evelyn and Darcy were there for the ceremony but begged off early due to Darcy's late shift.

Sam and family left the hotel a little early to get the kids home to bed. Little Victoria slept through dinner and Jason bounced from person to person till he finally dropped off in Dan's lap. Matt and Bruce took Mother and Daddy with them for a quick night's rest and then to the plane the next morning. Pam drove back with Geo and he picked up his car at Sam's and drove back to Boulder. With kisses all round, the room was cleared before seven o'clock.

We'd decided to put off a honeymoon trip until the early summer. Mosscreek was far from complete and I'd given notice that I would vacate my condo on or before March 1; the owner was anxious to list it. We had furniture decisions to make, movers to schedule and Cal had to get his office functioning.

I'd had an update that my security clearance was progressing and I would now be scheduled for a complete briefing on the "proper safeguarding of classified information on the criminal, civil, and administrative sanctions that may be imposed on an individual who fails to protect classified information from unauthorized disclosure." I gathered that George had been so glad to get rid of me that he didn't bother with any derogatory input. I learned anyway, that with Cal's type of security clearance and his involvement with the DHS, he had to take particular steps in order to leave the country so we would stay close to home for the time being. All in all, I knew that now with Cal, everyday would be a honeymoon, and I told him so.

In any event, we'd decided to take a chance and had purchased advance theater tickets for the Broadway show at the Buell Theater. With the curtain at 7:30, we'd just make it. We felt like kids running through our beautiful hotel suite, grabbing coats and a quick gulp of champagne, and rushing to beat the curtain. Some people would think that was not a very romantic way to start a wedding night, but in a posh, dark theater, professional presentation on stage, wonderful surround sound, and the one you love, now yours forever, close beside you . . . we believed we had chosen a winner.

CHAPTER SEVENTEEN

▼

Agnes McMullen arrived in Denver on March 21st, weeks after her brother's his subsequent wading through the impending legal matters. He had done very well to keep her in the dark. She was not informed of any details of the case and the basics, didn't know he'd only been out on bail, or that he had been kidnapped. When he'd disappeared, I'd been certain that she would show up at the rectory and all hell and excrement would have hit the proverbial fan. As it was, after her threatening call when he told her about the basic facts, she calmed down and felt secure enough to withhold her sisterly surge of dominance until she could get away; she apparently had a very busy life in Florida. As Mac said, "Thanks be to God."

John DeBeers was very fortunate to have a judge as kind and open to his needs as was Judge Contreras, and to have a prosecution team so willing to take all the extenuating circumstances into consideration and back off of their normal aggressive approach. It was apparent to all concerned that John had not completely adapted to his new lot in life as an amputee. It was also apparent that for their accused, life itself was an ongoing day to day struggle.

Under the auspices of the Court, DeBeers had been thoroughly examined by additional psychiatrists, both civilian and military. When he returned from Walter Reid Hospital, a second series of polygraph tests had been given and apparently every question he was asked provided a positive and truthful outcome on the chart. However, whatever the actual result, it was deemed that when the answers were compared, they were contradictory. I don't know what questions were actually put forth, but Angeletti said that questions about Father Mac turned out to be consistently truthful . . . on paper, even though Mac could not have possibly been involved in the activities that John claimed to be true. Angeletti continued to emphasize that in his opinion polygraph tests were not necessarily reliable since it was almost impossible to discern if the answers that appeared to be truthful or not on the chart could just as easily have been the result of a spike in the emotions, or extremely well controlled emotions, which he felt DeBeers could have handled if he so desired. For myself, I believed it had simply boiled down to the fact that the Magdalene's pushed DeBeers to the breaking point taunting him about his Saint John and flaunting their warped approach to faith and he felt responsible to do something about it and it had backfired.

As we learned in the past, his survival from his horrible experiences in the war zone, one in particular that cost him his legs and probably most of his sanity could not help but fill one with compassion. In a closed court hearing, John was released into the custody of his attorney and handed over to the VA hospital for further evaluations and treatment. At Father Mac's hearing his charges were dismissed due to lack of substantial proof or evidence; or something like that.

*   *   *   *

As I reported, the dreaded sister, Agnes McMullen, arrived. She had borrowed a friend's gigantic Chevy Suburban to gather her brother and his belongings. I'd helped him go through the storage unit where the church had taken all his worldly goods, few that they were. We sorted through them and had them boxed and ready to load into her vehicle and transport them and him to his new life in Florida.

His retirement had gone relatively unnoticed since he had practically been erased from the current event calendar of the church by that time, guilty by association or something like that. He was philosophical, "I'm a jailbird, now, you know. I had a pretty clean rap sheet but with those Magdalene's spreading their theories around, and how readily we all spread gossip, I guess I'm getting off pretty lucky just to get away from here; extra lucky to be moving into my own little condo and not some dreary retired priest's home. No more snow; only hurricanes, foreigners, and sunshine."

I took him out to dinner and had looked up a restaurant chain in the area where he would be living and gave him a fat book of meal certificates. I avoided any personal topic. He didn't need to know about finally settling the divorce with George, or that I had married the man I'd been fooling around with.

*   *   *   *

When Agnes pulled in to the storage complex and it came time to load in the boxes, we had our first stumbling block. She brought a list and she wanted to see with her own eyes that we had included the gifts she had provided for him over the years. "Where'd you pack the raw silk vestments I had made for him, the ones with the medallions embroidered by the nuns that I brought back from Rome? Where's the needlepoint cushion I made for his twenty-fifth that goes on his *Prie Dieu,*" (she looked at me as though I radiated *duh,*) "His Prayer Kneeler," she barked, "where is it?" I pointed to an object lovingly wrapped in packing blankets and then opened a box and showed her the cushion carefully wrapped in tissue. This went on until we'd assured her that the books were all accounted for as well as his Mass and Sacramental kits, his ordination chalice, showed her the packed sound system and all CD's the TV set, his complete wardrobe, coats and hats, and the brass desk items, wall pictures, and of course, his private cell phone so she wouldn't have to pay for a new one. Jeez! Mac wasn't destitute; he'd told me about his savings, he'd be fine!

His motorcycle trappings were the last things to go into the back. She wasn't too happy about those but he actually stood his ground, "I don't have a car, you know. This is how I get around now." (The owner of a local car dealership promptly reclaimed the loaner he always provided to the current reverend upon the first hint of a possible diocesan scandal.)

We'd rented a motorcycle trailer and the last chore was getting it safely locked onto the trailer hitch and the bike secured. It made me tear-up. A wonderful era was rapidly coming to a close. Mac had been a part of my life for what seemed to be almost all of my life. He'd been my friend for over twenty years.

CHAPTER EIGHTEEN

▼

Mac was safe, packed away, and gone but the events surrounding his mysterious kidnapping had still not been resolved. I'd received a positive response to my application to the Magdalenes and was invited to any meeting held on Thursday evenings at eight o'clock. The new Father Pieter had hired a new grounds man and had withdrawn the open key/open church policy from the ladies. They had only access to one small room with an outside door, the inner door to other areas now padlocked on the other side. They had to be let in for their meetings; no more free access to the church goodies. He had visited Father Mac and received an excellent overview of the Magdalene's agenda, such as he knew it. Poor Mac didn't even know the half of it that I unfortunately did. Father Mac was adamant that an excommunication procedure should be considered. There was certainly enough heresy or apostasy floating around that group to oust them permanently; their own female priest, I mean *really!* And ordained in Father Mac's vestments, and presided over her confessional, Magdalene's 'Mass' and worships . . . ? *Off with their heads* would be more like it!

Albert Angeletti, Esq. had been kept on retainer by the Bishop's office to continue to clean up all the loose ends and get police files closed. He asked me to visit with him a week after Father Mac's departure. It was clear that he felt he had to pursue the kidnapping and I was still on retainer myself. It was only that a sworn deposition regarding his ordeal had allowed Father Mac to leave, and then with the agreement that he would return for any trial or further actions as may be required.

Angeletti still wanted me to infiltrate the Magdalenes, this time though, for Father Pieter who had been instructed by the Chancery office to investigate the reports of their activities that Father Mac had brought to them. I was only to work through Angeletti, however. I didn't want to get caught up with another priest's problems.

We were both reasonably certain that they were behind Father Mac's strange kidnapping, and we were all as thoroughly confused as he'd been on the purpose of the entire scenario.

I didn't know if we'd ever find out any more about poor John DeBeers fate, but again, I was happy that I had never been directly involved in any area of that. I was going to have my hands full once Cal got his responsibilities in place with the Department of Homeland Security, (DHS for short.)

Mosscreek was now eighty percent complete. The new staircase and door to our new study had been stained and varnished and they looked as old as the originals in the main hallway. The painters had done a wonderful job with some hand-applied antiquing. I couldn't have been happier. My condo had been emptied, cleaned, and turned back to the owner. There was still work to do in Cal's condo, as we were still juggling furniture, bedding, household goods and personal items back and forth.

The mystery of the 'finding' at Mosscreek still troubled me greatly, but since reasoning with myself, I felt more saddened than afraid or uncomfortable. I mentally thanked Cal a hundred times over for keeping me completely ignorant of the location, or anything else that could be haunting me at this very moment.

I felt sorry that Clarissa had purchased the house and lived there until her old age and never knew of the terrible fate of the prior occupants. I knew that the sleuth in me was roaming around in the back of my mind. I was slowly growing stronger, emotionally and wanted to help them be put to rest. I wondered what happened to cold case files.

*   *   *   *

Cal's office was now complete. We had a DHS secure satellite dish that fed his computers and mine and a switch over that brought in world-wide television stations as well as a high-security tele-conference capability. He had several computers situated around his large horse-shoe shaped desk area as well as hand-held electronic devices that I'd never seen before, even on the latest Internet shopping sites. An installation team had flown in and wired and checked the security on everything, and delivered cell phones. Every thing in our office wing was fitted with high security technology. We even had a separate electrical panel and all the electrical outlets had electrical bleed-out protection; much like those in hospitals and surgical areas. They were all grounded together to prevent a voltage differential and to prevent electrical mishap. Cal was careful to be sure I understood all the security precautions.

I was hyper attentive since my intense DHS briefing that went over all my responsibilities and outlined very clearly the cautions involved with a security clearance. Believe me, I was now a long, long way from the innocence of that *StarWay* consultant!

My first assignment from Cal was to spend as many hours as necessary on the Internet reading everything and anything related to the Department of Homeland Security. Our computers had some sort of a block to prevent cookies and any sort of tracking or hacking. Since we were connected to that magical DHS network, everything we did online was recorded, tracked and stored. We had a separate home wireless network that ran my laptop, so I did my research there. It was strange that when I set up the laptop, in spite of the powerful wireless network DHS had installed, it did not register when I configured my laptop on our household wireless.

My 'mini office' next to Cal's has rapidly become my favorite place to be. Unlike Cal's view, my window overlooks the rear of the property. I can just see the bend of the little brook that wraps around to the front and side of the house. Tall aspen trees, pines, and Colorado blue spruce grow randomly in a mish-mash of untouched wilderness. I've seen a red fox and any number of deer and an occasional elk munching along the edge of the water. The desk from my condo fits perfectly under the window and I have new small file cabinets flanking each side, more for miscellaneous storage than paper trails. I managed to fit my bookcase in on the opposite wall, and brought up the small-scale recliner and reading lamp from my condo. Sometimes, due to different time zones, Cal works late into the night while I snuggle in my chair with a heavy tome or my *Kindle* content as a cat on a hearthrug.

$$*\qquad*\qquad*\qquad*$$

Everything, as least from my novice status and much to my surprise and dismay, I couldn't believe that so much information and descriptive details were so easily available online. Just for edification and future reference, I printed out pages on my private household wireless printer.

I got busy trolling around cyberspace I was amazed to read about the *Biometric Passport* in *Wikipedia* which is also known as an e-passport, ePassport, or a digital passport. I don't have one and I guess if we ever go abroad, since this is new technology, every security niche in the world will know about me. Actually, Geo would be getting one, I was certain, for his trip to *Riyadh*, I'd be very interested in examining it. Apparently, the Biometric passport is a combined paper and electronic passport that contains biometric information (identification of humans by their characteristics or traits) that can be used to authenticate the identity of travelers by using contactless smart card technology, including a microprocessor chip and an antenna for both power to the chip and communication. It's embedded in the front or back cover or center page of the passport. This technology is used for facial recognition, fingerprint recognition and iris recognition, and retinal scan. All critical information is printed on the data page of the passport and embedded in the computer chip. Some national identity cards are fully compliant biometric travel documents as set forth by the International Civil Aviation Organizations. There is another biometric identification out there; it's called 'biometric voice recognition.' Jeez!

As an aside, I ran across a couple of articles about facial recognition saying that many people don't know they are already on some facial recognition database. Apparently those in the know can capture your face off something like *Facebook,* or snap you even if you're walking down the street, (I hope mine was captured just after a visit to *Jorj's Salon!*) and then download it into a tracking application that will spit out name, address, family members, and even your shopping history. The problem that we have is that you can't prevent the collection of your image. While we can protest and lament the intrusion into our privacy there is little or nothing we can do to prevent it.

One of the more distressing finds came from an article about unmanned 'drones.' Apparently the Federal Aviation Administration has the authority to certify certain entities which permits them to launch and remotely control information data gathering drones that can be as large as an airplane or as small as a house fly. Some have the ability to attach themselves to a window and transmit back what they are 'seeing and hearing.' The article stated that while this technology may be new to most of us, the military has been using drones for over fifteen years. *Oh well, welcome to the world, Middy!*

There are so many governmental agencies I don't wonder that they clash sometimes and really big things can get lost in the cross-fire. In another area, and again according to *Wikipedia*, the *United States Visitor and Immigrant Status Indicator Technology* (US-VISIT) is a DHS immigration and border management system that involves the collection and analysis of biometric data, such as fingerprints, which are checked against a database to track individuals deemed by the United States to be terrorists, criminals, and illegal immigrants. US-VISIT is accessed by over 30,000 users from federal, state and local government agencies, but it seems to me that someway, scary ones still manage to slip in. Immigration officials have the ability to instantly check the person seeking entry against several "lookout" databases using the *Interagency Border Inspection System.* DHS has ten-fingerprint scanners at major U.S. ports of entry, again I wonder, how do they still manage to get through all these filters and cause chaos? From what I've picked up reading, and which is unsettling, is that for many, many years baby terrorists have been born to affiliated radical groups all across our country and now they are bona fide Americans by birth. I'm certain this has been happening all over the world, as well. The violence just keeps finding new ways to infiltrate what was once relatively secure; even if it was only in our minds. Tragically, our own countrymen/boys keep bringing their own loaded arsenals into public places and creating their own versions of mad carnage and daily forcing us to doubt everyone's sanity. We refuse to believe that there is no solution and that we'll find a way to make it all better . . . we're like trusting children in that regard.

Having tried to absorb all that, I realized how incredibly proud I am of Cal for wanting to move into this complicated but vital arena. If one continues to pursue the state of our country, it is impossible to avoid being overwhelmed with the constant behind the scenes activities going on to protect us. In spite of the more publicized and horrific events that slip through the cracks, there is a long, long list of terrorist activities, on the web of course, that outline the tremendous successes in thwarting the majority of those planned attacks in their infancy. I'm proud to be an American and part of the Free World as we all pull together to attempt, even though sometimes fruitlessly, to ensure World Peace, or even peace within our small corners of the world. Getting down into the nuts and bolts of it all is really getting to me. I guess we go through stages from panic to peace. How I wish, in my own red, white, and blue heart that we'd had a series of presidents and politicos less self-serving who actually believed in our country as much as I do. Obviously, I'll not be able to journal *exact* details of our work, but I think it's okay to say that we are going to be doing a lot of tracking of people on the government's 'hot list,' but we're only a small operation and everyone seems to be doing that these days.

Besides, I'm getting excited about getting the balance of Mosscreek completed, maybe even have a few guests by summer's end. I'm certain I'll have a few tales when I complete the renovation of Mosscreek and open either my B&B guest area, or the special events venue. I have a little time to think about which way I'll go, but people are so darn interesting that I just know I'll have something to write about.

CHAPTER NINETEEN

▼

As it turned out, one Thursday I was driving back in to Cal's/our condo and I had girded my loins, so to speak, to go into battle. Tonight I would be attending the meeting of the Magdalene's. I wasn't sure if I'd contact Angeletti or let it ride till I had a couple of meetings under my belt. I really hated to be put in this position even though I was going to charge him my regular hourly fee. I'd been spending cash like a drunken sailor (forgive me US Navy folks) on Mosscreek and the end was not yet in site. I have to save something for old age if I make it that long . . . sometimes I wonder!

I'd planned to spend a couple of nights and take Pam out for dinner the next evening. I hoped she'd stay over until Saturday morning and maybe go shopping with me for new linens. I had to get started getting the other bedroom wing ready for whatever I was going to do with it

My cell phone rang and I didn't recognize the caller. I answered it out of habit, 'Middy Brown.'

A hesitant and elderly voice was on the other end; "Oh, Miss Brown, you don't know me but I have a friend whose daughter used to be a *StarWay* customer of yours, now I know you don't do that anymore, but I'd like your advice if that is, if you could . . . ."

I pulled over into the cul-de-sac of a subdivision and took out my notebook. It seems she lives next door to the home owned by Johnny DeBeers' mother and she had some concerns. She said it was really almost nothing and she didn't want to talk to the police, and since I had . . . so forth and so on . . . would I have time to stop by and visit a bit. I jotted down her name, Eva Carson, address and phone number and set a time for the following morning. She was obviously very nervous to be bothering me. I'm always a sucker for a lead-in like that.

✴   ✴   ✴   ✴

Several women were waiting outside a lower door beside the church and I ventured over and made sure they were waiting for the meeting of the Magdalenes. Promptly at seven, a burly man in a Carhartt jacket and work pants ambled over and jangled the long strap of keys hanging down from what was probably a belt loop, and unlocked the door. The women poured in. "Finish up before nine, that's when I'm back to lock up," he cautioned and nodded politely and walked back into the shadows toward the parking lot.

By seven fifteen Mary Elizabeth had rearranged the chairs and tables to suit her and called the group to order. She asked if there were any visitors and I shyly raised my hand. She did the big, chest-puffed-out buffoon style welcome to be sure we all understood her importance and her holder-of-all-knowledge position. She asked for applause while she went over and bolted the door from the inside. The bolt looked new. I suspected its purchase had come from the Magdalene's operating funds rather than a kind installation provided by the church.

She started out by going over the old business, indicating that she was happy to see the members who had been hospitalized were now well and back in attendance. She asked for an update from those to whom she'd given assignments. One woman raised her hand and was called upon, "Sister, Sister Luella is still in the hospital because of the food poisoning at the meeting two weeks ago. Her diabetes continues to be unstable and is hampered by her obesity. Her prognosis is not good." Mary Elizabeth nodded and the woman sat down.

Another woman stood and waited to be recognized, "Ruby is likewise still in the hospital, she has pneumonia as a result of the sickness since her body has been so weak and she wasn't over the flu. She asked for prayers to *Divine Magdalene*." I turned toward the sound of a very loud snuffle. The young woman sitting next to the door had her hand over her mouth only half obscuring the expression of horror on her face; I was the only one to look around. *Why?*

Another started to stand, changed her mind and started to sit down again. The Leader saw her and barked, "Shirley, do you have something to say or not? If so, stand up and let's hear it and if not, for goodness sake, stay put!"

The slightly built woman near me stood and glanced around, a shy little rabbit trying to decide if it was safe to follow Flopsy and Mopsy into farmer McGregor's vegetable patch, metaphorically speaking. I had a sudden surge of pity. What was this little woman doing here? Her salt and pepper hair was wiry and damaged from a home perm, her shoes were scuffed and worn down at the heels, and I could see the fuzzy pills on the worn areas of her sweater. She spoke quietly, "I'm sorry, Sister, but I wanted to say that I had to take a bus home last week after our meeting. My front tire had been slashed. I would ask for a ride home from a sister, since I haven't been able to replace it yet. I had to walk several blocks in the dark to get home."

Whew, my opening. I popped up and waited for recognition (I was learning) "May I offer our sister a ride home? I'd be very happy to be of service."

Shy Shirley turned to me, smiled and mouthed a 'thank you.' Our leader nodded an assent. I was in! But, why didn't she comment on the poor sisters who had been hospitalized? What about the slashed tire? Didn't they care for one another, or were they too preoccupied with . . . what?

Mary Elizabeth then begin to talk about the new business which consisted of the conference in Houston coming up in early June, details were in the flyer she would be handing out, and that car pools were being organized along with lodgings with the Houston Magdalene's hospitality homes.

Perhaps Angeletti and I were barking up the wrong tree. If this group had a national membership like I'd seen and read, surely they wouldn't stoop to the abduction of an old priest that they didn't like . . . would they? And, they'd most certainly have a lawyer keeping them within their legal rights, shaky though they might be, and what was going on, anyway? A Houston chapter, or cult, or clan or what ever they called themselves was probably pretty powerful. I'd better get back to my homework.

I glanced around the room my mind clicking on what the first one had said, food poisoning? I was dying to ask for more details . . . how many were hospitalized, what had they eaten? Slashed tire? What was going on? I'd have little Shirley all to myself after the meeting. I hoped she'd open up.

Ten women were seated here and there at the tables, not appearing to be in conversational conducive groups or ready to engage in girl talk. Every woman was very stern and serious. This did not seem to be the place to make a wise-crack. Our leader took up the stack of flyers from the table in front of her and handed them to a woman sitting nearest the front. She took one and passed them around the room. I had to stand and take mine from the woman two tables away from me who seemed disinclined to move her butt for the good of the order.

The meeting rambled on. There was a brief video with some supposed Divine Sister giving her sermon about the virtues of womanhood, devotions to *The Magdalene,* and an encouragement to spend time in suffering and reflection. From my perspective, she sorely needed elocution lessons; I had to keep from nodding off. Half of her words were lost to me because she kept forgetting to use her lips to help her with the hard words.

After lengthy and rambling prayers, by the Leader of course, Sister somebody went to the back table and brought a tray of goodies around to the tables. Sister some one else provided bottled water. One would suppose this would normally be a time for casual chatter, however, all the sisters kept to their places at their tables and munched alone and silent. I dropped my cookie in my purse and made sure the water bottle was factory sealed and did not contain any suspect hypodermic pricks. Sister tapped her little gavel on the table and all rose, and chanted something about Blessed and Beloved Magdalene. If I was going to join, you'd think they would have at least handed me a cheat card with the words.

The Leader stood by the door and unlocked and slid back the bolt allowing us to exit. The burly man was standing on the small incline just below Father Mac's little Blessed Mother grotto that looked so cold, neglected, and abandon in the yellow light seeping out from the door. I felt a sad, cold fist close briefly around my heart. Little Shirley scooted up next to me and smiled. I wanted to say something but there was no sound except feet slipping and scooting along the sidewalk to the parking lot.

Once we were clear of the lemmings, which was where I felt I'd spent the evening, in a lemming pre-suicidal huddle, I spoke out, indicating the direction to my SUV. As small as little Shirley was beside me, I thought I'd probably have to boost her up. Actually, I was right; I also buckled her in before slipping back around to the driver's seat. Would this winter never end, already?

I smiled as I started the engine and pushed the heater controls up a notch. "Would you like to stop for some hot chocolate and a burger? I didn't get a chance to have dinner (I lied.) She clutched her cloth purse closer and I quickly added, "My treat since I'm new, I'd like to have a chance to visit."

She smiled and nodded, I could scarcely hear her over the blast of heat coming in from the multiple vents, "that would be very kind."

I convinced her to slip out of the warmth and go inside the twenty-four hour MacDonald's. It was clean and bright and I prayed it would be safe. Anymore you just don't know and that makes me very angry. Should you sit in the back away from the doors? Away from the windows? Eat in the car? Grab a bag and squeal tires getting home ASAP? I placed our orders and bravely joined little Shirley who had chosen a booth beside the concession counter. I grabbed stirrers and sweetener on my way by, sat down, and made small talk, long winter, cold feet, that sort of blather. When our food came it was as I'd expected, she didn't waste any time nipping in. I started the gentle interrogation and learned that the membership was falling off with now only those ten members plus the two in the hospital.

She sighed, "Since the murder none of us like to go to meetings at night. Some of the women are afraid of that big man that unlocks the doors. Sometimes Father Mac used to be walking the grounds at night and he'd walk us to our cars and make sure we were safe. Sometimes Johnny did the same. He was always such a nice man. Not everyone likes the way Mary Elizabeth goes on about him, but we can't talk about it. We all knew Johnny was not quite able to do everything. He was so quiet and those awful metal legs, we couldn't figure out why he'd even been given the job. They say he slept in the church when the weather was bad. Some of the older women said things to him that he didn't know how to take. I don't think he meant to kill Mary Martha, I hope God will forgive me for saying this but she was really mean and of course she loved to provoke him, and he a wounded veteran. I felt sorry for him. Since he's gone I don't think I will keep being a member. It's not the same, especially since all the mischief like the painted-up cars and my slashed tire; it is getting to be frightening."

She glanced around and I got us another cup of hot chocolate before commiserating, "Boy, those things make me think twice, too. Do any of the sisters group together like special friends? It seemed to me that they all seemed, well, quiet and maybe even lonely?"

Shirley shook her head, "Oh no, we're not allowed to get chummy or see each other outside of the meetings unless The Leader gives us a special assignment. We're really not supposed to talk to anyone else about our group either. We all take a promise to Beloved Mary Magdalene. I'm only talking to you because you are very kind and I believe that you need to know some things if you're going to join. It wouldn't be fair otherwise."

I stepped in, "I appreciate this so much. I do want to know what I'm getting in to. Tell me, do they ever do anything illegal, like take things for their use, or maybe try to get back at someone, like for instance, Father Mac? Mary Elizabeth told me that they really don't like him."

She kept gently blowing on her cup of hot chocolate and finally she answered, "I know what you mean, but I don't think so. See, if you did anything you'd have to do it yourself since you're not allowed to be with or talk to anyone else in the group. Maybe someone could do something bad because we're all human, but no, I think Mary Elizabeth just likes to spout off about things. She's really not cut out to be a leader like Mary Margaret, but she's still mean in her own way. I think to be honest, Mary Margaret was mean too, even worse . . . a lot worse."

I took another route, "It seems to me that somewhere in the publications, there was something about each group being able to ordain a priest, does that mean you let men in?"

She almost choked, "Good heavens, no! Our priest is the sister of Mary Elizabeth and the late Mary Margaret. She's Mary Anne, but we call her 'Holy Sister.' She can't come to meetings since she has to be sort of I guess, cloistered, you know, not mix with people and just pray all the time. She only comes to do the confessions and masses . . ." She frowned, "In fact, I don't think I'm going to go back to any more meetings. I don't feel good about some of the stuff anymore. I feel really uncomfortable when I go to church on Sunday. I get confused with the scriptures Father Pieter reads and then the way Sister Mary Elizabeth explains them the next week."

I nodded, "I can understand. I'm a bit frightened about the vandalism that you mentioned, and the food poisoning. What happened to cause that, have they decided?"

Again she shook her head. "It was the new sister's turn, Sister Beth, she was the one sitting by the door, the one that started crying again. That night of the poisoning, she cried and cried and said she hadn't done anything and that she bought the cookies at the *Quick Stop* in the shopette by the gas station on the corner. Anyway, as you heard, they all got sick. I don't like coconut so I didn't eat any, but everyone who did get sick had to have eaten either the coconut things or drank from the big jug of fruit punch, and I don't know who brought that. I didn't have any of that either, I don't like to have things that I don't know where they came from. It was awful, some of them started throwing up right away and then the ambulance and the police came, even the fire truck with the resuscitation equipment. By the time they left, the ones of us who were fine told the police what we knew and then were allowed to go home. That's when I saw that my tire had been slashed. I looked around to see if a policeman was still parked by the church, but no one was around anymore. People don't understand that when you live only on Social Security you don't have the extra money to buy replacements of things they vandalize. I had to pay to have someone put the spare on my car. When I got it back home, the old spare went flat. It's still sitting there."

My head was spinning by the time I left my charge off at her little duplex. As she had said, an old Chevy Nova was sitting on half of the driveway that separated her dual unit with the one next to her. Good Lord, something was going on but I couldn't connect it to Father Mac. I needed more to go on. I'd have to get away and ponder on it while I took a nice long soak in the jetted tub back at the condo while attempting to assuage my guilt for having been given such an elevated status in life.

CHAPTER TWENTY

▼

The tree-lined street where Eva Carson's little white and brick-faced bungalow was situated was akin to the similar ones flanking the quiet street, and like many of the older Denver areas. It was only a couple of miles or so from the church. I remembered that Mac once remarked that John DeBeers walked back and forth to work since he didn't have a retro-fitted vehicle to accommodate his handicap. During all of the examinations of the poor man, it had come to light that he had retired, medically disabled, as a full Colonel, which meant he should have easily had the funds to have about anything he wanted, yet why had he lived so simply? It had to be hard to walk that distance, why had he not been provided with a vehicle? I once had a customer with a prosthetic arm and even though it allowed her to do most anything, there was still often irritation on the body areas that supported it. He was becoming more and more a very enigmatic man. The world just got stranger and stranger.

I pulled into the driveway of the Carson home and studied it for a minute before getting out of the car. The front porch area had been converted to a sunroom and I could see a profusion of blooming plants through the window. It was a neat house, well maintained with brick steps and a brick walkway; both appeared to be newer bricks than the ones on the chimney at the side of the house. As I approached the door to the sunroom I could see two white wicker rockers with floral patterned cushions inside. I rang the bell.

The woman I took to be Eva Carson was a tall, large-boned woman with a no-nonsense demeanor. When I introduced myself, I found that the woman who answered the door was not Eva, but rather Eva's sister, Ida. Eva herself was pretty much as I had pictured, slightly built, tidy gray hair pulled up in a bun, and somewhat nervous. When I had been ushered into a living room that was a similar companion to the sunroom and given a seat on a floral sofa, Ida explained that Eva had invited her over to meet me and talk about Eva's concerns. Ida was apparently the mother of my former *StarWay* customer, wherein came the connection and the foreknowledge of my penchant for investigation.

After tea was poured and small talk completed, Eva began, "Now Miss Brown, I know you work for a detective, my niece explained all that, and we hope we can just call this a friendly visit to pass on some disconcerting information about the house where that murderer has been living. We can't afford to pay you anything." I assured her I was no longer involved in the PI business and would thus not require anything for my time.

She hesitantly shared her concerns after identifying the home of the late Mrs. DeBeers which was to the left of her own. I stood and glanced out the large windows behind me and it was clear that any and all activity at that house offered unrestricted visual access. With some more glances at her sister, she began her story. I took out my pad and took notes.

"Well you see, Mrs. DeBeers and I had been neighbors for many years, although not really close as in friends, more like a visit while puttering in the yard, or chatting upon a chance meeting. She invited me to tea on occasion and I returned the favor. She had a lovely home with many antiques that she pointed out had been collected during her husband's military assignments around the world. He had passed by the time she moved to Denver. Her son, John Jr. was third generation military officer and she was of course very proud of that fact. Other than those very few references to family, she never spoke of anyone else; which is why I became concerned when two young women showed up several weeks ago with luggage, a locksmith, and then promptly moved into the house where they have been since. They had Mrs. DeBeers' car towed away and then it showed up on the driveway a few days later and they've been driving it. It's a big old Chrysler, quite cumbersome I always thought."

Ida broke in, "I've been terrified for my sister, imagine, living immediately next door to a *murderer*! I've stayed over in the guest room as many nights as I've been able, just simply to assure myself that she is safe." Eva rolled her eyes.

I looked sympathetic, "Mrs. Carson, what is it that has concerned you to the extent that you think I might be able to clear up for you?"

She glanced out of the window and began to tell her story; "Well, you see how easy it is to see the house next door, as I said, those two girls just took over. There've been trucks from antique stores taking away some of old Mrs. DeBeer's furniture, and they come and go at all hours, hardly willing to give me a nod when I happen out in the yard. I believe they're home right now, so we'll have to be casual when we go outside and I show you what I've found."

The three of us trooped around to the setback between the two houses and Eva begin to gesture toward the foundation of the DeBeer's house. "Look closely, that was not there the last time I walked around to my back yard in the fall. Do you see that? And, look here at the other window, what do you make of that? It was never here before, of course now that the snow has melted down; it's quite easy to see. I tell you, it was never there before winter."

I leaned over the remains of a dirt-speckled, leaf-infused low snow crust piled below DeBeers basement windows. I pulled out my cell phone and took a picture, then moved to the other window and did the same. I gestured for us to leave and go back into her house. My heart was beating so wildly I didn't trust myself to speak. I looked at the photos I'd just snapped. There was no question. Faint but clearly visible in window one were the words *Help Me*, written in reverse; in the second window, very clearly rewritten *Help Me*. Father Mac . . . his abductors had been the DeBeers girls!

I quickly reclaimed my calm and smiled to the two women, "Well, it certainly is interesting. It reminds me of writing *Wash Me* on a dirty car. I think I'll just go next door and visit with the girls; I'll give you a call later in the week to see if there has been any other suspicious activity. For the present, I'm very sure you are quite secure. They're probably just cleaning out their grandmother's house now that their father is safely in jail. I wouldn't be too concerned. You said they're just girls?"

"Oh, yes, anyway, not much older than their early twenties; they're both rather large girls."

I gathered up my notepad and purse and assured them that I'd come back over if I felt there was any need, but that it all looked quite unthreatening to me. I thanked them for the tepid, weak tea and walked down the stairs. Panic. What to Do? Call Angeletti? The police? By the time I'd arrived in front of DeBeers house, my subconscious had taken over. After, I'm an assistant private investigator, retired. If I couldn't question two young girls, I wasn't worth my salt. I smiled and rang the doorbell.

*   *   *   *

The curtain next to the door fluttered but nothing happened. I stood quietly looking as pleasant as I could manage and rang again. Another long wait. The door opened a fraction and I spoke to the crack, "Ms. DeBeers? I'm working with the attorneys on your father's case. May I come in and have a word?" The door opened wider and she asked for some identification. I handed her my *CC Investigations* business card. The door closed. After another wait, it opened and I was ushered into the dimly lit living room. It was obvious the house was being vacated; at least most of the furniture was gone. There were no chairs so the one who introduced herself as Beverly asked me into the kitchen where we sat down. I glanced at the floor; old linoleum, and just beyond the kitchen table; a basement door. Beverly called down a hallway and a second sister came in. Beverly introduced her as Beth. My mind connected with my memory, Beth as in Magdalene's Sister Beth! She must not have recognized me. Oh, my Cow!

Now that I was in I had to immediately come up with a secure strategy, "I want to offer my sympathies for what you both must be going through. I never met your father, but Father McMullen has been a friend for many years. How is your father doing?" I had noticed the quick glance and rigid posture immediately upon the mention of Mac.

Beverly spoke, "Dad is doing fine; he has nerves of steel. He knows what he's doing. Anyway, it was self-defense. If the lawyers would listen to us, this would all be over by now."

This took me rather by surprise so I began to dig, of course, "It was my understanding that they are looking for a mental illness or PTS Syndrome defense."

Beth snorted, "They're all idiots, and he's taking them for a ride, that's all."

"I don't understand, I'm working with Father McMullen's attorney and apparently it was your father's statement that involved the priest at all. Is it possible for you to let me know what this is all about?"

The girls exchanged glances and Beverly shrugged, Beth took over, "Look, I saw you at the meeting of the Magdalene's last night, so I guess you are going undercover too. I haven't found out anything, how about you?"

"Beth, yes, of course, the one with the bad coconut cookies."

She spat out, "Dammit, I didn't do anything to those cookies, they were old and had bacteria, I can't help what happened. The Health Department inspectors said it was not my fault, they fined the store where I got them and anyway, why are you stalking the Mags?"

I smiled in my most confident manner, "We've all been concerned for both your father and Father McMullen. This is in strict confidence, of course, but I believe the Magdalenes to be a very strange group, possibly even dangerous. What is your connection if I may ask for clarification?"

Beverly got up, "Sorry, I need a beer, you want one? I nodded and she opened three bottles of *Corona* you know . . . when in Rome. I'd been doing a quick recon of the house when she let me in, so I hadn't checked out her footwear but now it jumped out at me. She clomped back from the frig in scuffed brown boots. Bingo!

Beth took a swig, "Same thing, Dad has me on stake out, and he thinks they've been trying to kill Father McMullen for quite some time; that's why he said what he did on his lie detector test. He wanted the priest arrested and kept safe in jail; he was afraid those crazy women would get to him otherwise. But then, they let him out on bail. Dad got really upset; he and the priest are really close friends."

I almost choked on my beer. I composed myself. "So, that's why you abducted him and kept him here in the basement; to keep him away from the Magdalene's?"

Now it was their collective turn to spew beer, with eyes about to pop out of their heads they said in unison, "How did you know?"

I took my turn answering, had a long draw of the cool, golden liquid and shrugged, "I'm a private investigator. Besides, he told me about writing on the windows of your storage room. You might want to clean that off."

They both jumped up and ran out the door. I casually looked around and relaxed, patting myself lightly on the shoulder. When they came back in they dropped into their chairs shaking their heads. "We never knew, never for a minute. He was such a sweetie. He was polite, quiet, and never made any fuss. After Dad got his attorney to listen to his story and got him to try to plead a case for self-defense, he said he'd told the attorney that he'd been deliberately false about Father McMullen and that he'd only been trying to see if he could get him in jail to protect him from the Magdalenes. When they released him, Dad really got worried because it would be easy for anyone to get to him. He told us where and when to pick him up and then where, when, and how to get him back when he believed it would okay again."

Needless to say I was flabbergasted. Talk about wasting time barking up the wrong tree all of these weeks; Mac's fondness for Johnny was certainly well founded, I practically stammered, "But, your father passed a polygraph test. It proved that he was truthful on all counts. I don't understand."

They laughed, Beverly cleared her throat and finished off her beer and took a deep breath, "Ms. Brown, our father is a decorated highly disciplined Colonel in the Army. He has been in hundreds of situations behind and in the middle of enemy lines; he's been a prisoner, gone directly into battle deliberately leading his troops straight to the front lines; he's saved lives, been wounded multiple times, and when his Hummer was hit that last time, it flipped and turned over; burning and filled with smoke and still under fire, both his legs were pinned under the front end, he was in excruciating pain but he still tore off part of his burning shirt to make a tourniquet to stem the bleeding of the officer in the back seat, then he held his driver in his arms until the poor kid on his first tour stopped screaming and died. All the while Dad was losing blood and his flesh was burning. Do you think that sounds like a man who couldn't stay calm and say anything he wanted to and not pass a lie detector test? It was easier for him than when he was captured and underwent water-boarding. *Duh!*"

I felt like I'd been dropped on an alien planet, where had I been that I knew absolutely nothing! I pressed on, "You said he is pleading self-defense, then why are the attorney's going so strongly for the mental incapability?"

Beth answered this one, "Because Post Traumatic Stress Syndrome is such a great cop-out. I'm not saying his attorney is not the greatest, but he has to prove to everyone that Dad isn't loony so he has to go that route till Dad's cleared of the implications. Okay, so he loses his temper and he's been really upset that he accidently killed that Magdalene bitch . . . my word, not his. He feels really guilty. He's killed a lot of people but like he says, 'that was war; this was just a stupid, misguided woman.'"

"So," I asked, "how was it self-defense, he broke her neck, and from that very first minute he began to implicate Father McMullen?"

Beverly took over, "He said that Mary Martha leader person found out that he spent a lot of time in church praying. He does novenas and prays to Saint John, his patron saint. He still prays all the time, even in jail; someone sent him some beautiful medals and prayer books about Saint John and he almost called it a miracle. He prays for Mother, for us, for the governmental leaders, for the world, for the innocents of war, for everyone but especially for Mother. She's in the final stages of Multiple Sclerosis. She made him leave her because she refused to let him see her as she declines. She has a lot of other medical conditions, that's why she's in such bad shape. He pays for full time care for her, he pays our living expenses and he pays for our college. Ever since his accident he's never had a fair break. We're all lodestones around his neck and he doesn't care, he still keeps praying and taking care of us. We don't think he should have let Mother have her way, but when he was around her she cried all the time because she said she couldn't stand how much her illness caused him pain. You'd have to know Mother; anyway, he let her have her way but he agonizes over it. We keep him posted all the time and he wants to be with her at the end if she wants it or not; now he's got this jail or prison thing haunting him."

"And the night the Magdalene woman was killed," I prodded.

Beverly got herself another beer and stood by table, "That was one of those horrible but unavoidable and instantaneous reactions that happen that you can never take back. Dad said she'd locked up the church and he'd finally decided to take matters in his own hands and get back her key. He'd observed them that night and they'd done some deliberate and disgustingly sacrilegious rituals and he knew that Father McMullen would want him to get them out of the church immediately; Dad was going to tell him about it the next morning. When the Magdalene woman was leaving, he approached her and told her what he'd seen, and said on behalf of Father McMullen that she had to turn over her key. She laughed at him and started swearing. She said some horrible things about the priest and Dad as well. She told him to just watch out because the priest was a dead man and they had it planned so no one was going to be able to stop them. He said she was stomping across the snow on the way to the parking lot and he tried to follow her. He said she turned around and started taunting him about not being able to walk in the deep snow and that he was a waste of a man and a worthless cripple and an idiot as well. Then she tried to knock him down with the big purse she was carrying. At first he tried to block her blows but then when she came closer and was trying to push him to the ground, he grabbed her arm and they started slipping. She kept swinging and he lost his balance. He said it was probably instinct but he inadvertently locked his arm around her neck in a futile attempt to stabilize himself when they both started down. She twisted and he held on to keep from hurting himself in a fall. When they both hit the ground, even though the impact was mildly softened by the layers of snow, he heard her neck crack and knew immediately what had happened. He said he cursed himself, his worthless body, his injuries, his stupidity, the horse of a stupid woman, and the world. When he'd calmed down and what she'd said about Father McMullen came back to him, he knew the mentality of the group and felt terror for him. He wanted to find a way to keep the priest away from them. He said after that, he called Father McMullen, the police arrived, and then they drew their own conclusions so he decided to let things take their course."

We were all silent for a few moments, I asked, "What are your plans?" Beth said they were emptying out the house and had sold off the antiques and a realtor would be coming as soon as they were finished. They'd worked with the VA and now had the additional money necessary to have a SUV retro fitted for their father's handicap. As soon as he was released, and they were both positive that was only a matter of a short time, the vehicle would be ready and they were all going back home to North Carolina. The Durham VA Medical Center would be close and would take care of all their Father's needs. They'd help him find something to keep him occupied. He said he was going to get involved in a program that helped wounded warriors learn to live with themselves.

I was still reeling when I thanked them for clarifying so many things and asked them if they would repeat their story to the attorneys if I scheduled it. They were both very happy and eager to comply.

The meeting was scheduled and I sat in Angeletti's office during the time they repeated word for word what they had told me. I thanked them all and told Mr. Angeletti that I would forward my report to him. He walked me to the elevator and I must say, he was quite overwhelmed at what I'd been able to accomplish. Modesty disallows me from repeating his comments. It was over. I was done; the rest was up to the law.

CHAPTER TWENTY-ONE

▼

It was May, at last. We were settled into Mosscreek, Cal was deep into his work, and as yet, there was no final word on my Security Clearance so I took the time and enjoyed the leisure of retirement. I wanted to do some landscaping and Benny had hired a tough young man to help me relocate some rocks and do some digging.

I started just beyond the little gazebo. I thought I'd level a space and put down flagstone to create a level seating area. I envisioned a staging area in the gazebo for everything from weddings to lectures, to a musical venue. It was late in the day and my helper, Eddie, had moved all the rocks and piled the smaller ones into a loose-laid wall that bordered a small grassy knoll. We had raked and shoveled most of the area and my level space was coming along well. I sent Eddie home and since Cal would be tied up for a couple more hours, I rested on our 'engagement' rock and finished off the thermos of tea. I decided to work a little longer and so I shoveled down an area that had been under one of the larger rocks and tossed the dirt over and behind the new loose-laid stone wall. I'd removed a couple of feet of dirt when I tossed a hunk of dark material over the fence with the dirt. I leaned over and retrieved a crusted and moldy fragment of leather. I went back to the hole and dug further, uncovering what appeared to be a suitcase. On my hands and knees I put on my gloves and kept digging. Within a short time I had discovered a case about three feet long and about two feet wide. At the edge of my excavation was a strap of leather with two rusted clasps and a hard U-shaped handle.

I sat back on my haunches, breathless from the excitement of my discovery as well as from exhaustion. I studied my discovery; faded fabric protruded from the area where I had dislodged the leather fragment. I had a sudden chill run up my spine and goose-bumps the size of walnuts pop out on my arms. I stood, dusting the mud and dirt off my gloves and jeans, and looked around. The forest had become eerily quiet; ultra quiet, no bird calls, no breeze, and only the faint rippling of water behind me from the creek. Suddenly a cold puff of air floated over the top of the wall and seemed to surround me, and uncontrollably my goose-bumps crawled up and around my back and neck. A stone rolled off and landed at my feet. I took a deep breath and watched the tall grasses just behind my dig area swirl gently back and forth for a nano second and then the puff seemed to dissipate. The silence was almost palpable; I think I may have heard my heart pounding. I pulled off my gloves and laid them at the far end of the wall on my way back to the house, leaving the task of completely unearthing the find to Cal. I didn't want anymore decomposed bodies on my conscience.

Back in the kitchen, I found Gracie busy at the stove. I'd forgotten that this was one of her nights to prepare dinner. I now remembered that she'd volunteered since she knew I'd been spending the past few days working hard on the grounds and she wanted to be involved in some way. I went into the maid's room and took advantage of the bathroom to scrub off most of my accumulated soil and pull the scarf off my hair. When I got back to the kitchen she had poured me a glass of wine and was sitting at the table snapping fresh peas.

She smiled, "I have to ask you to forgive my forgetful mind. I never did finish my story about our Miss Bonforte; seems like it just came to me again, real powerful like."

My eyes widened, the goose-bumps were back again, what was going on . . . I chugged a mouthful of wine and rose to refill the goblet, "Oh yes, you were going to tell me about the *troubles*."

She nodded, "Yes, I 'spect they've been on my mind all day today. It took me back to that other May and all that happened what changed everything, I imagine you'd like to hear about it."

Of course, everything else fell away from my mind, the strange episode outside, however, still lingered. I shivered again. Clarissa was always a top priority expecially when I was here. In fact I was wondering earlier, prior to my discovery which I had now convinced myself was nothing more than an old trash dump, that I hoped she would have liked having us live here and would have approved of the additions we'd made to our beloved Mosscreek. Gracie was ready with her tale.

"As I said, it happened that it was May, just like now, and Miss Bonforte was in love. On Friday nights she would hold them gatherings when her friends would read them poems, or stories, or what not and everyone would have a gay time. As it were, there were a fellow what came every week, and I must say, me and Benny didn't take to him. We was really concerned when him and Miss Bonforte started walking out together, as Benny had caught him out back with one of them fast gals and they was doing what they ought not a' been doin', and they was enjoyin' it just fine, according to Benny. We didn't know just what to do as we purely loved Miss Bonforte and would never step out of place, so Benny thought he'd have a talk with that young man. Well, you know it; he just laughed and said all manner of nasty things to him. We felt helpless. Poor Miss Bonforte, by the end of the month, she confessed that she was in a family way by that man and that she loved him the whole wide world and that they was to be married when his folks was to come to Denver. Well, you know how that went. They never did come and he was full of excuses. To our heartbreak, he moved into Mosscreek with her. That was the second *trouble*, the first being his own self. Well, he treated us bad and sometimes she scolded him, but she was blind to everything. Well, before anyone knowed what had happened, he claimed to have got drafted and had to report. Well, she was heart broke and begged him to marry before he left. He give her a big story about President Truman needin' him, and he would come back from Korea a big hero and she'd be proud to become his wife then, but he wouldn't budge about marryin' her beforehand. He was excited, like I 'spose any young man would be at the thought of defending his country. Anyways, he never did come back and she never heard from that sorry fellow again. She locked herself upstairs and didn't come down for days. We left her meals outside her door and then took them away and left a different one the next day when she hadn't answered the door or ate a bite. I took to sleeping here in the maid room and checking upstairs through the night hoping she'd show her face. When she finally come down, she didn't talk and looked terrible bad. Everyday she looked worse. I told her she could be hurtin' the young'un, so she'd drink a bit of juice or take a bit of porridge, and then go back to her room."

She sighed heavily, "Course, the writin' was on the wall. Her time come in September durin' the night. I was right here, ponderin' about what me and Benny should do when I heard her screaming. I went to the phone and cranked it up and Benny come runnin'. There weren't nothing nobody could do. She had give birth to a tiny little dead baby. Not knowing what to do, I fixed her up as best as I could and give her something to help her sleep. I didn't know what to do about the babe and when I asked her, she moaned *I don't care, just bury it in the woods*. Well, Benny fixed up a little box and the next day we went back into the trees behind the house and dug a tiny grave. We said prayers and marked it with a tall rock. Clear up to the day she died she never mentioned that night, the man, or the babe. I suppose that was the last of the *troubles*, but she never again had one of them poet nights and she stayed on here alone, writin' her poems till she went to live at that old folks home where you met her. She'd only drive into downtown Denver in that big old car to meet with her book people once in a while. She stopped being happy, quite wearing fancy clothes, and let Mosscreek bring her the peace she needed. She loved me and Benny, though, and we was able to get her to laugh sometimes. She'd walk in the woods with them big old dogs, course the first set of 'em was long dead, she kept replacing dogs, always needin' to have their comfort. But she always carried a lot of sadness. I wisht you could have known her and been her friend. She would have loved you like me and Benny do."

CHAPTER TWENTY-TWO

▼

Over dinner I told Cal about my long talk with Gracie. We were both saddened to learn of all the sorrow that must have haunted Clarissa for so many years. Then to change the subject I told him about the object I had partially unearthed during my outdoor project. I had decided that it was probably just an old trash dump, and that if he would be free in the morning, I'd like to dig further. Like the private investigator he'd been most of his life, his eyes lit up. "Middy, darling, have you dug up another sleuthing opportunity?" He smiled. I had to admit, since our move here to Mosscreek, it seemed as though those smiles were far more relaxed and frequent than they'd been in the past. I know he was very happy to be out of the line of fire, literally, from unknown assailants . . . or known ones for that matter. Actually, so was I. It had never occurred to me those years gone-by that I'd ever be on the receiving end of danger; ignorance is bliss. I laughed and realized how very wonderful my life was turning out to be; we were quiet a happily settled-down old, comfortable pair.

I casually remarked in reference to my sleuthing, "Well, actually I do miss snooping around a bit. I have to admit I felt like someone walked over my grave when I saw that buried *something* in the yard. Everything went eerily quiet and I had the uncanny feeling that something had drastically changed. It made me shiver and reminded me about something I've wanted to do. Do you think it would be possible to research our home here, maybe see when it was built and who initially constructed it before Clarissa bought it? I've been visiting with Gracie and I'm rather intrigued. From what she said at one time, the house was partially furnished when Clarissa purchased it and some of the older pieces were already here, but she said she didn't believe anyone had actually lived here before Clarissa moved in. See, you know me well enough to know that I already read a lot into that. Now that I'm over the initial panic of what you found upstairs, I'd like to put my mind at rest and see if I can get to the bottom of our mystery. I have the distinct feeling that what I found may be connected. Why would someone bury a leather case?"

He went to the kitchen and came back in with the coffee carafe and refreshed our cups before returning to the chair across from me, raising his eyebrows in that old familiar way. "I've actually been mentally counting down to see just how long it would take you to move into another unknown arena; I know my girl." He laughed, "It's not dark yet. Let me get that portable spotlight and let's go outside and unearth your find. I can't imagine your Clarissa burying anything in the yard, but whatever it is and whoever is responsible is intriguing. At least we should put our minds at rest. Otherwise knowing you, my love, you'll lie awake all night making up stories about its owner. Don't expect me to hold back a few chuckles if it's full of bones and fur from a departed four-legged friend. Gracie did say that she had dogs."

I shuddered, "I don't look forward that, why would anyone bury a dog in clothes and inter them in a suitcase?"

He held up his hand, "Hey, Clarissa is your mystery I'm just hanging on for the ride."

I sighed, "Morning is soon enough to find out what it is. Maybe I'll refrain from accompanying you. In fact, maybe we should just ask Benny do it."

Cal laughed, "Whoa, gal, I've been around you and your intuition way too long to let you get away with passing this one off. I'll be ready in the morning with the shovels."

✳   ✳   ✳   ✳

I pulled on a heavy sweatshirt and jeans and ran downstairs in my wool socks. Cal was nowhere to be seen. I smelled the wonderful wake-up aroma of coffee and padded into the kitchen. Cal wasn't there but I noticed that he'd set out my insulated mug so I quickly filled it and then went to the bench by the kitchen door and laced on my working boots.

The morning was cold as it is in the foothills of Colorado in May. As I suspected, he'd become caught up in my mystery and was sitting on the rocky wall in the sun, shovel at his side. He smiled as I approached and I made my way over yesterday's dirt piles. I saw that he had excavated further and had opened up more of the area around my find. Now it was easy to recognize it as a piece of disintegrating luggage.

I studied it for a moment before taking a seat beside him on the wall, "So, why would someone bury their luggage with clothing inside?"

He shrugged, "Perhaps I've connected to your wave-length. I feel uneasy about it as well. Why indeed? You have me wondering if there is even a remote possibility that it is related to the upstairs find. I can't decide if we should bring it to the surface and investigate, or make a call to the sheriff and ask him what he thinks. I suppose it could be part of the mystery, as remote a possibility as it seems or if after all this time, if it is related, that there would be any actual evidence that could be lifted from the object, prints or something of the sort."

That same cold shiver I'd felt the night before sent goose bumps the size of eggs up my arms; I jumped up and threw my arms out wide, "Everything around here seems to have an underlying story! I mean, when you think that somewhere behind us in the forested areas there is the grave, yet to be found, of Clarissa's poor little baby. And you're right, who knows what else has happened here? Why didn't the people who built the house and partially finished it never move in? Why did they sell it to Clarissa leaving the antique pieces behind? We should get a couple of items appraised, I know they are really very old, almost from the Italian Renaissance, if my internet surfing is on target. When Matt and I were here that weekend, she swore that that tall divider at the end of the parlor is a *Wayborn* Italian screen divider, probably circa early 1300's; the same with the Italian Credenza across from the piano; you know her, she knows her stuff. Anyway, seems those two at least would have been too valuable to leave behind." I sighed in frustration, "So, whatever you decide I'm with you, I just can't put that little niggling in the back of my mind to rest. What shall we do . . . dig or call?" I caught my breath. Cal patted the rock where I'd been sitting before I'd jumped up and started raving. I sat down and we tried to make some decisions.

In the end we decided to go in and put together breakfast and when it was a reasonable hour, Cal would call the sheriff who had answered the initial call and get his input. The sheriff told him that he saw no problem in having us complete the excavation, taking care to preserve any evidence and contact him if we believed anything we discovered could connect the contents to the upstairs find. He then referred him to the coroner's office where he said additional information had been discovered about the victims.

Since it appeared that Cal would be spending the balance of the morning on the telephone, I busied myself with straightening up the house, clearing up the kitchen as well as my mind, and popping some laundry in the washers. Did I say how extremely convenient it is to have multiple washers and dryers? I knew they'd be busy most of the time when we opened the house to guests. We just hadn't had time to actually make final plans in that area. In the mean time, I enjoyed the luxury of excess.

The chicken salad I'd put together for lunch was resting in the frig when Cal finally joined me in one of the oversized rocking chairs on the side veranda. He was shaking his head and smiling. "You're going to freak out, my dear. We have some very interesting information that has just come to light about our victims. I almost hesitate to give you this additional fodder to ponder in your very fertile mind."

My mouth dropped open and I was aware of actually salivating. "Don't keep me in suspense! First of all, can we unearth our find?"

"Yes, the sheriff said to use all precautions in the event it may be related to our upstairs guests. We are to preserve as much, in tact, as possible and call him if anything useful comes to light."

"And," I queried, "the other information?"

He sat back, amused at my instant excitement, "First of all, we ran into a bit of luck. It seems a young woman doing some sort of internship with her work in forensic science was given permission to do some graduate work through the coroner's office on the skeletal remains of our victims. She has released her report and has determined the age, sex, and ancestry of the victims. The assistant coroner I spoke with said that even though the case may never be solved because they have only the skeletonized and some fabric remains to work with; he explained that the forensic anthropologist is often the victim's last chance for identification and justice, but in this case it was doubtful if they'd ever obtain any further information than what she provided. It's a very cold case and there are no reports of missing persons within the surrounding five hundred miles from the early to the mid 1900's that fit the gender mix that we have."

"What did she find out; do we get a copy of the report?"

He shook his head, "I didn't ask about a copy, but I don't know that it would give us any further information. She found through some DNA testing that they are all of one family. The eldest male was in his late thirties, the woman middle thirties, the eldest child, male was about four, and the girl about three. They were all of Italian ancestry and all alive when they were shot in the same location they were found. There were traces of a *Quicklime* type substance that inhibits odor while slowing the body decomposition found on all victims. The date of the simultaneous deaths occurred somewhere between 1935 and 1940 according to her best estimate, which may be off due to multiple factors."

For a few moments neither of us spoke. Finally I emitted a very sad sigh, "What a horrible find, and in our house. Who were these people? I was just talking about Italian furniture and now we find that an entire Italian family was murdered here in our home. Perhaps Gracie was wrong. Maybe these people did live here and became involved in some sort of a disastrous association. Cal, I have to research the house now, and I pray that mysterious case in the yard has nothing to do with anything but a garbage stash."

He ruffled my hair, stood and stretched, "At least we've received some information that may eventually help bring this to a closure of some sort. Let's grab some lunch and get together some containers for our dig. I told the sheriff that I'd keep him apprised of our finding."

CHAPTER TWENTY-THREE

▼

Cal went out to the barn to see what he could locate for our project and Gracie called telling me that they wanted to go to the big theater at the Mall and catch the early movie. They'd stop at the supermarket on their way home and if I'd give her a list, they'd shop for us as well. I happily agreed and rushed through the pantry and frig and by the time they arrived in the circular drive, Cal was digging and I ran out with the list.

Benny got out to investigate Cal's project and I asked Gracie a question that I'd had on my mind, "Gracie, do you know how Clarissa furnished the house, I mean apart from the furniture that was already her own?"

She pondered a moment or two, "Well, ya' know, she'd already been living here a few weeks when me and Benny come to work for her. From what I recall, her daddy, now remember he'd give that girl anything she wanted, anyways, her daddy let her have most of the things they had in their house in Denver as they was spending most of their time at the ranch in Texas. She said at one time that they wanted her to live in the house and let her get any furniture she wanted, but she declared she couldn't think in the middle of a busy city. I recall she'd mentioned that three or four of the bedrooms was already set up, and a piece or two in the parlor. I know she brought what she could use and bought other things to put everything to rights, as she said. I don't recall that she ever said what all was theirs or what she bought on her own. I know she said she wanted to have everything comfortable like she'd had at home."

I replied that I was curious about the Italian screen in the parlor and Gracie said Clarissa's mother 'like to have died' when she saw it, so I 'spect it was already here. Miss Bonforte loved it and said it would always remind her of the time she visited Italy. She'd been practically all over the world, though. I imagine some of them other real different-looking things was also from her travels, like that dog statue piece in the entry. You know, all of her dogs looked just like it. They was lovely creatures, too. Always right there next to her."

"Gracie, what happened to her dogs?"

"Oh, lands, they lived forever, it seemed. One by one when they past, she were already a getting to be a old lady herself, but she kept getting new ones clear up to the end. They's all buried in that pet cemetery just behind that Veterinarian hospital where you turn off the main road. Oh lands, she had a funeral and flowers for each of them just like they was her own flesh and blood, she even visited the graves often times."

After they left I couldn't help but wonder if she ever paid her respects to that other little grave hidden in the trees.

*   *   *   *

Between the two of us, we managed to ease a tarp under the case and carefully lift it out of the hole and onto the flat ground. It was in surprisingly good condition and held together well. Piece by piece Cal lifted out the rolls of fabric and placed them on another tarp. At the bottom of the case we found two pair of men's shoes, one an expensive black dress shoe, a couple of leather belts, pair of evening suspenders, an electric razor, and several bottles of aftershave lotion and cologne. Obviously, items more recent than the time span of our upstairs people.

Cal carefully unrolled a man's dinner jacket, pleated shirt, bow-tie, two pair of men's trousers, a vest, three pair of men's briefs and two undershirts. All of them were in surprisingly good condition. He sat back on his haunches and looked at me, "Any thoughts?"

A picture had begun forming in my mind of a handsome, arrogant and most inappropriate suitor who had ingratiated himself to a young, impressionable Clarissa, left her pregnant with his child, and claimed to have been called away with a somewhat credible story, never to return. I could see a lovely, tear-streaked face and trembling hands burying the remnants of her love as dead as the child she had delivered. I respectfully asked Cal to replace the items in their case and leave her pain to where she had relegated it, to remain forever buried. Cal later called the sheriff and told him we had nothing to report.

*   *   *   *

Over the next few weeks my day laborer and I completed the landscaping, placed the balance of the flagstone on the area for patio seating, and had the gazebo repaired and painted. I was very pleased with our progress and my hastily planted pots of flowers were blooming in the warm June sun.

Samantha called and asked if we were open for business as one of her friends was desperate to find a place for a small garden wedding. Cal and I smiled and replied, "Sure."

The caterer arrived to view the kitchen area, the bride arrived to ooh and aah over our venue, and we accepted overnight B&B reservations for the four families that would arrive the day before the wedding from out of state. The pastor was duly impressed and asked if we would be open to additional functions. We gave him the number of guests that we were willing to accommodate, and before you could say 'rehearsal dinner' the wedding had come and gone. Samantha was thrilled that we could accommodate her friend in such luxury. We set aside separate rooms for the bride's use and designated the downstairs' maid's room for the groom's men, and provided each with champagne and small hors d'œuvres. We called Gracie and Benny back into service for the first time and they couldn't have been happier.

We packed our new chairs away in the barn and sighed in relief that what we had been postponing, as in, deciding what we would do with our wonderful house, had evolved entirely on its own. Cal leaned back on the loveseat in our little parlor with a sigh, "My dear, I believe you could be a success at anything. I really had no idea we could put on an event so effortlessly or lovely. I'm very proud of you. I think Clarissa would have been extremely proud of all that you've accomplished here in her home."

I smiled, "I almost felt her here. The guests adored the fact that this had been her home. The little cards you came up with giving her the honor and her home the exposure were an excellent idea. Adding the names and date of the wedding couple was a flash of genius. See, you are quiet the perfect lord of the manor yourself. To simply say that you know your way around a graphics program would be completely insufficient, you've set precedence; now you'll have to do this for every occasion."

He shrugged his shoulders, "Anything for you, my love, just remember we are no longer going to put ourselves in the time crunch we've lived in for so long. The Department of Homeland Security work comes first and always; don't even think of booking an event when we're in the middle of something. I know that may be hard to do, but let's think long and hard before we jump off another cliff . . . promise?"

I just smiled, my old boss was back and I was Middy Brown, assistant P.I. again. I meekly smiled, "Yes sir, I understand; now how about I mix us a couple of drinks and come sit next to you. I need a cuddle."

CHAPTER TWENTY-FOUR

▼

True to my promise, I made sure that the stack of 'must-dos' on my desk had been cleared up before I headed into Denver to start my search on the original owner of Mosscreek. Actually, it was almost too simple. A quick check on building permits for the periods of the 1930's to the early 1940's and property titles and transfers told me that a Carlo Barzini had constructed our house in 1938, and that a Clarissa Bonforte had purchased it in 1950, and that the title had been transferred to a M. Middleton Brown, i.e., yours truly, in 2009. All dutifully filed, recorded, and completely legal.

My next task was to find out something about Carlo Barzini, assuming that I could uncover the mystery of why the house may have remained unoccupied for twelve years before Clarissa came on the scene. I reckoned that he may have been thirty-something during its construction, which would put him pushing up the daisies or else, still hanging on at well over 105 or so . . . which could still be possible, though improbable.

After a quick lunch, I trotted to the offices of The Denver Post newspaper and hoped to gain access to the old microfiche files and records for the past sixty or so years. I was given an escort to the 'morgue' and instructions regarding research, and along with several other history snoops, I settled in for a long session. It was nearing four o'clock when I had my first break. A rather long obituary notice jumped out of the page for a Salvatore Barzini.

Longtime Denver resident **Salvatore Barzini,** owner of **Your Family Bakery,** died peacefully in the arms of his family on July 31at the age of 83. His beloved wife, Isabetta León preceded him in death in 1942 as did his eldest son, Carlo who died in 1940. He was born In <u>Mazara del Vallo</u>, Sicily in 1866 into a family of fishermen. He arrived in the United States at the age of fourteen and went to work in his Denver family's Italian restaurant in old North Denver before establishing his own enterprise. He was very proud of his fine children; sons, Carlo, Alberto, and Louis Barzini; daughters Angela Magaddino, Tita Pinzolo, Dolce Roselli, and Lucia Como; he was the grandfather of Pia and Maria Barzini, Tony Pinzolo, Lolli Como, and many nieces, nephews and devoted friends. A rosary service is scheduled for Wednesday at five o'clock at The De Santis Funeral Home. A Mass of Christian burial will be held on Thursday, August 4, 1949 at 10:00 in the Denver Cathedral, His Excellency The Right Reverend Bishop Thomas Marino officiating. Pall bearers, Augusto and Francisco Roselli, Tomas and Dumo Pinzolo, Paulo León, Tony Barzini. Honorary pall bearers: the León brothers Bruto, Carlo, Jacob Jr., and Louis.

There he was, Carlo Barzini, the owner and builder of Mosscreek, dead at the completion of his project; I could imagine any number of scenarios. Now I had far more than enough information to try my hand at locating relatives that may be able to give me some further history of Mosscreek. I realized that it was common to Americanize ethnic names, but I'd just keep my fingers crossed. I shuddered as I waited for the copy to print out. Our upstairs victims were also Italian . . . surely none of them were family members! With that many people listed in the obit and sharing the ancestry, I already knew from preliminary research that many of those surnames had been commonly associated with the Pueblo *'Black Handers* and the *Colorado Mafia.* Briefly I was wondered if I wasn't stepping into quicksand again. Only a few inquiries, I told myself, nothing harmful in that, right?

After about twenty telephone calls to surnames in Pueblo and Denver, I discovered several family members, but only three were willing to give any further names that I might try in order to make contact with a local Barzini.

Finally, I found one who was willing to chat. A somewhat youthful informant answering the phone to at the Italian Bakery *Pinzolos* said 'yeah, he has an Uncle Louie Barzini who is 'probably a hundred' but his dad couldn't come to the phone and I'd have to call later. I asked a couple more questions and he asked me to hold and he went back to talk to his dad. When he came back a short time later he said that he'd better have someone else call me. I gave him my cell number which still came up on the screen as 'Middy Brown,' so that's how I identified myself. I've found a bit of comfort in that previous identity.

About seven that evening, I received a call back from a woman who identified herself as Pia Barzini-Como and wanted to know why I was looking for relatives of Carlo Barzini. She was somewhat short and demanding and I became immediately uncomfortable. I quickly told her I was doing some research on my home and discovered that a Carlo Barzini had built the house and I wanted to just get some basic information about him to put in the history of my house, the one, I told her to avoid confusion, that's just up into the foothills west of Denver.

The tone of her voice changed and she hardly took a breath as she gave me the information I was looking for. "Oh that, yeah, I seem to recall there was supposed to be a house up there somewheres. He's long dead. The only one left who would know, if he'll talk to you, is great-uncle Louie. He's in a nursing home and his mind comes and goes, but he'll talk your leg off if he's in his right mind. Anyways, he's ninety eight and living in a place in old North Denver, close to what's left of the Italian section where we all grew up. We try to go see him once in a while, but you can't count on him knowin' who you are. You called my brother Tony, he don't know nothing about that side of the family anymore. I'm about the only one who cares and I don't care much, so he told me to call you. I can tell you where to find Uncle Louie if you want. It's best to just drop in the late morning, that's probably when he's the most sane. I wouldn't take anything he tells you as the gospel truth, though. He's usually got TV and his real life mixed up."

Needless to say, after two weeks of trying to ferret out a contact, I gave myself a pat on the back. Cal had been in D.C. working on a new project and wouldn't be home for another week. I couldn't believe that an old man in a nursing home could possibly be a threat, so I saw no reason to postpone my visit to Uncle Louie.

*   *   *   *

True to Pia's directions, I found the facility with little difficulty. It was an ancient stone building that had been remodeled multiple times without losing its old world charm. The grounds were beautiful on the late June morning and several residents were enjoying the gardens in wheel chairs and walkers accompanied by a number of staff clad in navy scrubs. I climbed up the central worn stone staircase and noted the long, gradual ramps that sloped down each side of the broad front terrace to the walkway and circular drive area. The carved double doors were embellished with beautiful beveled glass and the arch above boasted a stained glass window depicting Jesus in the Garden.

I pressed the bell and a woman in a smart dark suit and warm smile invited me to enter. Her hair was gray and cut quite short and she had a soft completion that radiated beauty without the use of make-up. The cross emblem on her jacket and her sturdy, no nonsense shoes added to the equation that said 'nun' to me. I gave her the reason for my mission and she led me to a room where I was asked to wait.

A few minutes later, during which time I took note of the severe furnishings and lack of personal items or softening embellishments, an older woman entered, dressed exactly as my first with the exception of a small fabric scarf, i.e. nun veil, clipped on top of her similarly trimmed gray hair. She extended her hand in welcome and with a friendly smile and with a well modulated voice she acknowledged me.

"Welcome, I'm Sister Carlotta, Mrs. Brown," (I still used my other official name when in my sleuthing mode) I understand that you are interested in gleaning some information from our resident, Mr. Louis Barzini"

I mirrored her smile, "Yes, Sister, I have a home in the Denver foothills that I've discovered was built by a Carlo Barzini, deceased, who was the elder brother of Louis. I open my home to small events and would like to give my guests a history of the house since is quite lovely and the former home also, of the late poetess Clarissa Bonforte. It is my hope that he will be able to give me some information about the original family or anything that would add to my project."

"I see, well, I'm happy to tell you that we have quite a history attributed to the generosity of the parents of the Barzini brothers, Salvatore and Isabetta León Barzini."

Startled, I thought immediately of Cal's chiding 'beginner's luck.'

We chatted briefly and she was happy to discuss her knowledge of the Barzini family, "We have a small historic ledger that records the Barzini family's involvement with our facility. They lived scarcely a block away from our facility, which was once a small private hospital. The father, Salvatore, so the story goes, became very saddened when he learned that the hospital would be closing due to financial difficulties. In those days, several elderly nuns were residents and there were no similar care facilities locally available that could accommodate them. One of those nuns had been the sister of Salvatore. He stepped in and provided the financial means to update the building and turned it into a home for elder clerics, most of whom did not have a dedicated facility provided by their own order. In later years, his wife, Isabetta, became extremely ill and he brought her here to spend her final months under the care of the staff of physicians and nuns. After her death he had the front of the building remodeled and the Italian stain glass window installed in her memory. Upon his death, we were informed that he had endowed us with perpetual funding to oversee the financial needs of our home here."

After another brief exchange of information and expressing my thanks, Sister phoned for a staff member to escort me to Mr. Barzini's room. The blue clad staffer quietly entered and a few seconds later returned to the hall smiling, "He is having a good morning and is happy to have a visitor. I hope he will behave, he has quite a reputation." She smiled and turned back down the hallway. I slowly entered the room. It was quite large and furnished in the manner of a lovely bedroom and study with a large carved headboard that somewhat disguised the hospital bed under the velvet comforter. The sun was bright and I saw through the double French doors out onto a small balcony. A voice called out, 'come, come.' As I crossed the room I noticed a computer on an ornate desk and in a corner beyond the bed a treadmill and several weights of various sizes on a metal rack. A large velvet upholstered recliner sat beside the left French door next to a lovely side table. A quick glance picked up an antique lamp, a modern CD player and headset next to a stack of audio books. This was a far cry from the Golden Care Center I once frequented to visit my *StarWays* customers.

Mr. Barzini was a small, scrawny fellow resting in a plush patio chair with his feet on an ottoman. He wore a smart work-out jacket and sweats in bright red and put his cigar in an ashtray on the table next to the chair that held a thermos and half a cup of black coffee. He reached for his walker, but I quickly asked him to please stay seated. He smiled and extended his hand in a warm handshake. He gestured to a side chair the staff member had most certainly brought out for me from somewhere in his large suite and I sat.

"Mr. Barzini, it is so good of you to see me, I hope I'm not interrupting anything."

He smiled broadly, his tan face certainly lacking the degree of wrinkles and age deterioration that one would expect to be associated with one of his ninety-some years. He still had a full head of gray hair that was neatly trimmed and combed and his eyes were clear and the color of the remaining coffee in his cup. He wore an incredibly ornate antique gold and jeweled crucifix that was resting on his chest and attached to a heavy twisted rope gold chain that disappeared inside the collar of his jacket. I introduced myself and told him the reason for my visit.

He emitted a hardy laugh, "No interruption here my dear lady. After my breakfast I work out and then when the weather permits, I'm right out here soaking up as much vitamin D as the Lord allows. Afternoons I listen to my books on CD and then nod off till they bring my dinner. I don't socialize, you see. I don't go to the dining room, hate to see old people fat and out of shape that never took the time to take care of themselves, you know, and now all they can do is talk about their ailments. So, I have lots of spare time to converse, especially with a lovely and intelligent person."

I laughed, "Excuse me for being bold, but you look amazing."

He adjusted his position and sat up straighter, "Used to run up Pikes Peak regularly down in Colorado Springs till I wore out my knee replacements and the doctors wouldn't replace them again. Now I have this walker to push around, guess it goes with the territory. I can still do a few miles a day on the treadmill, but I have to hang on now; damned old age." I shook my head in amazement.

We talked a bit about the view from his private little balcony. He insisted on ringing for coffee and sweet rolls and we settled in to enjoy a bit of silence and laughter. Finally he broached the subject, "So I was told you want to know about old Carlo and that house you bought?"

I hurriedly mopped the crumbs from my mouth, "Yes, I'd like to know the history and if there's anything you remember I'd love to be able to fill in the lost years of my house's history, that is, if you don't mind sharing."

He laughed again, "No, the old days were the best. I expect it was Pia that put you on to me," he laughed again, you're gonna think I'm a real bastard when I tell you that I do anything I can to keep her and that snotty-nosed bunch of grandkids of hers from coming here every Christmas to do their duty visit. In fact, I don't like no family coming here; I don't even try to think of who anybody belongs to anymore. I don't even know who they're talking about and they try to let me know that so and so is the nephew of such and such, shit, I don't give a damn. Hell, every damn one of them have had so many kids I don't even know how many generations have dragged in wrinkled new babies for me to kiss and how many have been named after me. I finally told Pia to pass the word around that I'm leaving all my money to the Planned Parenthood bunch so they'll always have money to hand out birth control to Italians."

We laughed together and he continued, "Hell, I started drooling and talking like I'd been traveling and had people off TV coming to see me and finally they got the message that I'm crazy and they dwindled off till now only poor Pia tries to keep up the pretense of caring about me. Anyway, what do you want to know?"

I laughed before revealing my mission, "When I did the research on my house, I discovered that a Carlo Barzini was the builder, but from information I put together, apparently no one lived in the house and it was finally sold in 1950 to a young poetess. I guess it's sort of a mystery and I became intrigued. I want to print out a little publicity-type history flyer to give to the guests who hire me and my house for their weddings, or other functions."

He shook his head and finished off his coffee, appraising me with raised eyebrows. He finally laughed, "Ho Boy! I haven't told anybody about that mess in my entire life, I guess since everybody but me is dead it can't hurt now. I need to be sure that you'll keep the family dirty laundry out of it if I tell you what really happened . . . otherwise, I don't know . . . ?"

Frowning I said, "I don't understand, Carlo Barzini is in public records as the builder of the house, anyone can get that information, but of course I'd never reveal any private information. I've got enough secrets of my own!"

He clapped his hands in enjoyment. I was really starting to love this little guy. "Yeah, yeah, I don't care about public records, hell the whole family is in police blotters from here to Chicago, I want to tell you what really happened because now that I'm just now remembering it, it's a hell of a story and I haven't thought about it since the old folks died. I think you'd enjoy it. In fact, I'm gonna order you a lunch plate so we can take our time. I like you, Mrs. Brown."

"Middy, please call me Middy."

"And Louie, call me Louie."

With that settled and lunch ordered, he began, "Well Carlo, he was the eldest brother and a real funny kind of guy, you know artistic-like, always drawing; the old house, a broken fence, the bell tower of the church, stuff like that. Now the Old Man had started this bakery business before he even got married and was making a lot of money. By the time us kids came along, he was shipping boxes of crackers, millions of those skinny little Italian breadsticks, *Grissini,* that restaurants are crazy about, that kind of stuff. All of us kids had to work in the bakery, help with the baking, deliver boxes, clean up the place, learn the business, so to speak. I think only one guy carried on the tradition I'm told. Tony somebody, one of the grandkids or in-laws, I don't know. Anyway, Carlo was a bit of a sissy-boy. The other kids all teased him, dumping flour on him, putting dough down his pants; he was fighting all the time and the Old Man couldn't stand having all the fuss. He called Carlo in and gave him a special job of delivering boxes to keep him away from the rest of us. He'd take the old delivery van and work and make deliveries from clear up to the Wyoming border down into New Mexico. Everybody wanted boxes from The Family Bakery, especially since they were actually often filled with bootleg whiskey. Carlo caught on somewhere along the line and started shorting a few shipments and leaving them off at places he'd contacted and pocketing the money. Of course, the customers that got shorted complained and Carlo got shipped off to college in Chicago to live with an uncle. Of course, that was fine by all the family since he was a pain in the butt to us all.

"Now our grandfather on the other side of the family was Jacob, *Big Jake* León. Our mother was his only daughter out of six sons. The sun rose and set in Jake's little Isabetta, and he had taken a liking to her eldest son, that being Carlo. When Carlo got out of college he was a pretty good architect and had a good handle on construction so he never got involved in our own family business. So now, the plot thickens, Big Jake León runs a great big *family business* of his own if you know what I mean, down there in Pueblo where the León family always lived. He decides he wants to take Carlo into his own business to oversee all of the property he owns and maybe make him, Big Jake, that is, look more legit seeming as how he was big into the protection racket and the big boss of his own *Black Hand* operation . . . do you know what that was?"

I nodded my head, "Yes, I've done a lot of research into Colorado's history. I certainly am familiar with our Colorado Mafia . . . that's what we're talking about, isn't it?"

He laughed and took my hand, "I told you, I like you! Anyways, the Old Man, our own Salvatore steps in; see, he and Jake never got on. Oh, Jake threw a big Italian wedding with all the trimmings for his little daughter, but it was only because she was pregnant and said she'd kill herself if he didn't let her marry her only love, Salvatore Barzini. She grew up in the business, she knew her poppa wanted to take him out, waste him, you know, send him to sleep with the fishes in the Pueblo Reservoir, but he wouldn't cross his little girl. Anyhoo, the Old Man does a one-up on old Jake and takes control of Carlo, like right out from under Big Jake's nose. He puts a house trailer for an office on the land where your house is and says to Carlo, '*We're gonna build a big house for your Mamma, someplace where she can get away in the mountains with the girls, like a vacation home. You don't tell nobody, it's a secret, you got any problem with that, you come to me . . . get it? You tell nobody, when it's done, it will be my surprise for her for her big birthday.*'

"So, Carlo, feeling like a big shot, moves to the foothills and draws up this big house, He's back and forth to the bakery, showing the Old Man his plans, making changes, and getting everything ready to go for the big surprise, which is about three years away if he was talking about our mother's fiftieth birthday. None of us knows what's going on except that Carlo has a new job, still we see him coming and going at the bakery. Us kids weren't dumb. We knew all about the uncles in the dark suits that got together and the women who kept making big spaghetti suppers while us kids all got sent over to some aunt's house. Funerals happened all the time. Kids wasn't allowed go to some of the funerals, and believe me, there was a lot of them, family members or not. Once we figured something big was happening with Carlo, we kept clear and didn't ask questions. We was street smart and knew what the score was. We was born knowing to see and hear nothing and most of all, to keep our noses clean and mouths shut. The Smaldone kids lived just a block or so over from us on Osage Street, what we didn't figure out for ourselves they taught us, they were our best educators . . . you know that name don't you?"

I nodded and raised my eyebrows but refrained from answering by a knock on the door. The same staff member came in to clear away the lunch and was surprised that I was still there and questioned Louis to be sure he wasn't tired. I think she frowned at me a bit when she turned her back on him to leave. I ignored her.

He leaned closer to me and motioned for me to close the French doors before he continued, "So, now's when the shit hits the fan. The house is all done, our mother's birthday is coming up, The Old Man tells Carlo to go on ahead and go work for Grandpa Jake in Pueblo and that something has come up and he can't get everything arranged for mother's birthday, but Carlo is now under a *sworn oath* to keep the house a secret.

Now me, I'm graduated from college a full fledged accountant and business manager and takeover the care of all the bakery's books. I ain't no dummy; I answer to the auditors and IRS and keep our noses clean and butts wiped, if you excuse the expression. My office is just off the Old Man's big private one. I was a pretty tough little guy; black belt, marshal arts, boxing, all that stuff, so I was pretty much in the protection racket myself . . . my job was to protect the Old Man both where the books were concerned, and his own physical self. I kept a few guns handy; you just never knew what might happen . . . those were tough times. I heard everything that went on and always kept my mouth shut, just like I was supposed to do.

"So anyways, off Carlo goes to work for Grandpa Jacob in Pueblo; but, Carlo smells a rat . . . so a month or so later, he drives back up to Denver several times to check out the house and he's discovered that a man, woman, and two little kids are living there and it ain't no family that he's ever seen. He stays around Denver on weekends, seeing his old pals, the Smaldones, and driving out to the house a couple of times. He hides the car, climbs the wall and finds an observation place in the trees. Sure enough, the man works around the place chopping out weeds, raking dirt, and in general, cleaning up around the place, landscaping and what not. When the woman comes out; she talks to him in Italian, the little kids play around, throwing dirt clods falling down, bawling, kid kind of stuff. The woman is young, very pretty, and stays close to the kids. Carlo decides to hang around and see if he can figure it all out. He thinks he would have known it if a family had been hired to take care of things.

"Now part of the whole project was a place for someone to live in a gate-keeper's cottage to be sure no unwelcome people got in, typical Mafia deal; so Carlo decides to take a few days off work from Grandpa Jake and hides out there. The gatekeeper place is locked like he left it and no gatekeeper has been hired yet. So, he grabs a few things, sleeping bag and food, hides his car in some of the heavy trees, climbs over the rock wall, and lays low."

By this time my heart was beating so hard I was afraid I was going to collapse. It all fit . . . my God . . . the family in the closet!

He continued, "So the tale goes, the very first night Carlo stays in the place he wakes up to car lights and someone unlocking the gate; it's eleven o'clock. He watches and sees none other than *the Old Man's* car drive up to the house. He slips out the back door and creeps up among the trees until he can see the front door. Sure enough, there's his very own father opening the trunk. The man comes to the door and helps him unload half a dozen bags, sacks, and boxes. He gets close enough to figure out it's a delivery of groceries. The woman comes out, he takes her in his arms, kisses her, and they go inside. A light upstairs comes on. He stays until two in the morning."

My host was getting more excited and asked if I minded if he lit a cigar, of course, he can do whatever he wants, I smiled and say its okay. He lights up and continues, I selfishly hope he will last until the end of the story, I'm not certain I can contain myself much longer. He asks me to get a couple of glasses out of his desk drawer and a bottle of scotch. I worry a bit about being an accessory to surely a very huge infraction of the facility's rules, but comply, bringing back only one glass and declining one of my own. He motions to me and I pour out a snort or two. He downs it and motions for me to return the contraband. I do. When I resettle myself, his hands are shaking as he puts the old cigar back in his mouth to relight, the lighter wobbles but finally he puffs and continues.

"Now, Grandpa Jake's no fool. He wasn't one of the most successful mobsters in this part of the country without making sure he was always covering all his bases. He trusted no one, and even though Carlo was his favorite of Isabetta's boys, he was still afraid that Carlo might be what you could call a double agent . . . working for Jake, but taking information to Salvatore about his covert operations. So, when Carlo starts leaving Pueblo so often, Jake gets worried and has Carlo followed. This particular night, Jake's man is not far behind Carlo and he sees what's going on and makes the same conclusion as Carlo has. The next morning they both drive back to Pueblo; Carlo to digest what he's seen and knows he has to keep his mouth shut, Jake's man reports to his boss and tells all. Now the story takes a strange twist; the next week or two when Carlo can get away again, he drives out to the house . . . no one lives there anymore. He still has his set of keys from construction so he goes into the house. He looks around. The furniture that had been delivered when the house was completed is still there, the kitchen is empty, pantry empty, cupboards empty. He can't figure it out. He decides the people were setting up the house for his mother. He leaves without looking around anymore and forgets it. Mother shortly after that develops a series of illnesses, Carlo forgets about the birthday surprise since she is now bedridden most of the time."

I was sitting on the edge of my chair, waiting for the end. He puffed his cigar and leaned further back in his chair and shifted his legs, changing their position on the ottoman. After about three minutes he looked at me, "Oh, are you still here?"

Startled, I stammered something about taking up so much of his time, and began to rise. He laughed loudly, "Hey, stay put, I'm just giving you a hard time. You haven't been listening to an old fool reliving old times without waiting to get the cherry on top of the sundae, have you girl?"

Again, I stammered about taking up so much of his time and began expressing my thanks when he put his hand on my arm. "Here's the end of the story, the best for last.

"You know how I said that Grandpa Jake didn't want Salvatore to marry his darling daughter, and that he would have had him taken out except for Isabetta; how he was always paranoid that Salvatore was going to horn in on his operations?"

I nodded.

"Well, you can see that if the opportunity came up, Jake would be most happy to get back at his tormenter. The Old Man was known as *The Padre* to everyone near and far and was well aware that the swords on both sides were kept sharpened, so to speak. As it turned out, Jake had started a little investigation on his own and found out that the people living in that nice, gracious home that had been build supposedly for his darling daughter, was actually a hideaway for *The Padre's* mistress, her brother, and *The Padre's own two children born of the blissful union*. Now Jake must have been equally furious and elated at the same time. He couldn't believe that the bastard who took his little girl away from him had done this terrible thing to her behind her *and* his back, not that he didn't have a harem of his own hidden away somewhere, but now he saw how he could get his revenge!

"He sent some of his men out to the house to get rid of them all and make sure no one ever found the bodies. They cleaned out all personal items and erased every trace of the four of them. Then the icing on the cake was that good old Grandpa Jake *forced Carlo* to go to our father and tell him what *Big Jake* had done; and so he did. I heard it all. After Carlo left, the old man went to pieces; he threw things, came in and demanded one of the guns, and tore out. He was gone for the next week. The day after he left, Carlo was found dead of a gunshot to the head. They called it suicide, but I never bought it. Carlo loved himself too much, but, who knows? I know the Old Man would never have killed his own son, at least I'm pretty sure he wouldn't have, he probably tried to have it out with Grandpa Jake . . . mystery unsolved . . . did Grandpa Jake have him put out to keep from talking? I only know when I came in to work one morning the Old Man was back working at his desk, unharmed, and the gun was back inside my locked drawer . . . still loaded . . . . so, who knows? To this day, nobody knows. Of course Carlo's death and the circumstances were altered in order to break it to Mother, but after that, she never recovered and died a few years later right here in this room that he had fixed up for her; and he lived with a broken heart, so they say, anyway, he was never the same. He knew that I knew the whole story, had heard the whole story, but he never mentioned it and here I am telling you, a complete stranger our family's dark secret. I have to swear you to secrecy . . . it would do nothing but harm the living that's left, and there's nothing anybody could do about it now. Do I have your word?

I stammered, "Oh, my goodness, I would never reveal all of this to anyone but my husband. We both live in the house, and you don't have to worry about him, or me for that matter; we're both retired private investigators, and we certainly know about keeping confidences."

He reached out and took both my hands in his, smiling. "Good girl, we'll consider that episode closed, Middy dear. That's the end of my story and I've pulled on your ear far to long for a first visit. You'll come again, won't you? I am confident you will only say that the house was held in trust for many years upon the death of its builder before it was released to be sold to your poetess, the more savory items would only distract from the peace and serenity I think you're trying to surround your little corner of heaven with, am I right?"

As I nodded in affirmation my mind was reeling. There I was, should I or shouldn't I tell him about my closet? I struggled a while with those two little images sitting on my shoulder. One said that I would upset him with the details, the other said he had a right to know . . . after all, he didn't have to air the family's dirty laundry . . . what to do? I told him.

He sat there quietly after I'd made my revelations rolling his cigar in between stained, crooked fingers gazing out over the grounds. After a while he reached for his walker and I stood and moved it over to him. He slowly used it to pull himself up and stood a moment, flexing his legs. He turned to the doors and I opened them, he motioned for me to follow. He went to his desk and pulled out the long flat pencil drawer. Taking out a business card, he handed it to me. "Call Adolpho, he's my lawyer. Give him the name of the coroner's office where the remains are being held. Have him make arrangements to have them buried in the family section under the name of Barzini, 1938; no other information is required on the marker. It's the least I can do for my father, he suffered enough."

He took my hand and kissed it, "Please come again, I hope this hasn't upset you too much. You should love your house. It was built by love for love; maybe just didn't turn out like it was planned. This is a good end to a sad story. I'll wait for your visit. Next time let's play a game of chess."

I kissed him on both cheeks in the European manner. We both had tears in our eyes. I drove back out to my home, my Mosscreek, seeing it with new eyes. I would ask the lawyer to let me know when the remains would be interred. I wanted to attend, and take flowers.

Chapter Twenty-Five

▼

Cal came back home from DC full of vim and vigor. He was excited about his new DHC assignment and said the powers that be were very pleased with our combined work. He said his friend would like to meet me and I'd been invited to accompany him in the early autumn when he was due back. I thought a trip to DC in the fall would be wonderful. Cal said we could take time away to drive through the hills and enjoy the beautiful autumn colors and take in a museum or two. We'd still never managed a honeymoon, but hopefully, the rest of our lives would become an ever-rewarding and never-ending beautiful honeymoon. You can't argue with that.

We drove in to Denver for dinner and a show, on the drive in I told him about Louis. We agreed that it was a peaceful closure of a traumatic time in our lives and the lives of the parties involved. He laughed and said he never would have believed that I'd actually stepped right into the middle of the Mafia and hadn't been shot at or kidnapped. I told him that he should be very proud of me since I stayed close to home this time and didn't have to have him rescue me. He laughed and gave my fingers a kiss. He turned to wink and said that rescuing me had always been half the fun. I punched him lightly on the arm and unbuckled my seatbelt so I could snuggle for a couple of miles. What a guy. Did *I ever say he'd been a really good catch?*

End

Books by M. Louise Smith, available through Amazon and all online bookstores and some downloadable as Amazon Kindle and other e-Book sources. Read on for more information:

<u>Texas Fictional Sagas:</u>

The Pact
Torn Shadow eBook: Accidental Wife

<u>Amateur Sleuth:</u>

The Middy Brown Journals
Journal I—An Appointed Time
Journal II—In Due Season
Journal III—A Time for Everything
Journal IV in progress

<u>Spiritual:</u>

Sonlite: Script—Novel coming in 2013

Texas Fictional:

The Pact—hardcover, paperback, (Kindle e-book coming soon)

Frank McNeill, a young architect and grandson of a contemporary of Frank Lloyd Wright finds his family's security as well as his honor and loyalty challenged by an evil far beyond his imagination or control; an evil orchestrated by an unlikely nemesis, Ishmael, a foreign student in Frank's University of Texas Crowd. Ishmael, the heir apparent to the Islamic tribe of Kuhmaad is the only one who knows of Frank's apparent murder of a prostitute during his graduation party. Frank's panic to conceal this act forces him to supply information to Ishmael for his hired terrorist so he can infiltrate the ranks of Frank's grandfather, Jasper McNeill's, International *Gateway to Freedom* project, where he has been contracted to make a kill. Ishmael is unaware that the man has additional contracts to eliminate all the high profile international board members including the president of the United States. Ishmael believes his hired terrorist is only going to follow his instructions to complete his assignment, the honor killing of a high ranking but dishonorable member of his family tribe. Frank realizes too late that he alone must avert the horror he has unleashed and unwillingly assisted.

Fan Info: *Barnes & Nobel reports that people who bought* **The Pact** *also bought: The* **DaVinci Code**, **Angels and Demons**, *and* **Deception Point** *by Dan Brown,* **Big Bad Wolf** *by James Patterson, and* **The Rule of Four** *by Ian Caldwell, Duston Thomason.*

Torn Shadow—hard cover/paperback/ Kindle eBook:

Young cousins, Scotty and Skeeter live in a dusty, dry family compound in South Texas. At the center of their world are grandparents Miz-Maw and Big-Paw, who keep the family together with a combination of love on the part of Miz-Maw, and a good dose of respectful fear on the part of Big-Paw; fear now mixed with horror since they've hidden in the thicket and witnessed the execution of his swift and brutal justice. When they find Skeeter's dog, Runt, gnawing on a decaying human arm, they become ensnared in the reality behind folk legends of the Brush-Bogey and the Conjurin' or Hoodoo Woman who is alleged to cast spells and even kill with her Evil Eye. Their gruesome discovery brings them into direct contact with the living Brush-Bogey who begins stalking them. Within days they are taken to the shack of the old woman where she forces them to carry out her horrific plan. Since they've witnessed the murder committed by Big-Paw, they are certain he is involved in the death of the owner of the decaying arm. Their vow to keep their silence places them at the total mercy of the Conjurin' Woman and her abhorrent scheme.

Women's Fiction

Accidental Wife—Amazon Kindle eBook: ISBN 978-1-61364-179-8

Estelle Fischer was young, beautiful, a debutante, and engaged to a rising NFL star football quarterback, but that all changed in a horrific second when she became responsible for the accident that brought her dreams to an abrupt end. Now, at age sixty-two and finally able to attempt to reclaim her life, she returns to the small compound of beach bungalows on Texas Gulf coast, just a mile away from the scene of the accident. Now widowed and the mother of four difficult adult children, will she be able to recapture any of what has been lost by arranging a reunion of all the old friends that she so abruptly left behind? Included in the list are her first love, now a Vietnam vet, her fiancé a retired sports hero, and the gathering of girls that have grown into troubled women. Her adult children believe that she has taken leave of her senses.

Amateur Sleuth:

The Middy Brown Journals I, II, III, (IV in progress)

(For the gals who have been there and done that . . . in other words, the slightly mature woman, sorry, no porn.)

Middy Brown Journal I, An Appointed Time ; also

Middy Brown Journal II, In Due Season—hard cover/paperback/eBook:

What is it with Middy?

Just about the time she's certain that she's mature enough to work side by side on a daily basis with Calvin C. Cleere of *CC Investigations,* the dreamiest and most available PI on the planet without losing her head . . . or more . . . her absent, cantankerous and chauvinist husband, George, complicates everything by filing for a divorce.

Just when she thinks her life is finally her own, her air-headed mother leaves her patient father and comes to live with Middy and begins to date. Her latest conquest could possibly a serial killer in search of another wealthy wife.

Just when she thinks her *StarWay* business and work for Cal is all she needs in her life, she encounters a nun on a dark highway who claims to have had an apparition!

And . . . *Just* when she thinks she can't possibly be pulled in another direction, one of her *StarWay* clients could possibly be the kidnapper of a very popular and charismatic television chef.

Middy Brown Journal III, A Time for Everything

<u>Middy Brown Journal IV, Cast Away Stones</u> *Coming in autumn of 2013.* How can Middy possibly not respond to the request for help made to her by a young Native American woman when she laments that her beloved grandmother has lapsed into what she believes to be a past-life regression. Can it be possible that Grandmother has become a channel for one of the four wives of the great Southern Cheyenne peacemaker; *Chief Black Kettle*, Moke-tavato, possibly the wife named Arapaho Woman whom he is said to have married in 1830? Grandmother claims she is being called by three of his seventeen children, sons, Black Kettle, Gentle Horse, and a daughter, Wind Woman. Is Grandmother, one of the beloved old people of the Southern Cheyenne, being called to heal a wound or a heartbreaking error from the past? Was it the fateful Sand Creek Massacre, or where the Chief and his wife met their deaths at the hands of Colonel George Custer in the battle at Washita River?

Spiritual:

<u>Sonlite</u> (script) Available for film/television option (Novel version in progress)

In a time of crisis, two women embark on the unpleasant task of bringing their apposing lives together in order to close out the past and each find a new path to help them move on with their lives. Mary, an unhappy, angry Caucasian woman is forced to give up her teaching career and return to a farm home she despised in order to close out the affairs of her deceased and bankrupt father. Martha, the elderly African American woman who has lived at the farm as Mary's father's caretaker finds herself in danger of being removed and made destitute by the other woman's prejudice, anger, and money woes. During a prayer service at Martha's church, in desperation she sends out a petition to the Heavens to send some Sonlite into her dark, dark life. The night Mary tries to burn down the farmhouse and kill herself, the beautiful young Black man who apparently appears out of nowhere seems to be the answer to Martha's prayer. To her extreme concern and consternation, she tries to keep herself from believing that he just might be the Son of God.